Praise for Jean

"The most distinctive voice of his generation and the master magician of the contemporary French novel." —*The Washington Post*

"Writing lives! Echenoz's words are full of grace and surprises, and he has the ability to throw relationships among them just off-center enough to make the images or people they convey seem all the more compelling and fresh." —*The New York Times Book Review*

"A gentle tending to perversity links Echenoz to that other master of the perverse detail, Vladimir Nabokov." —*Los Angeles Times*

"Echenoz seduces his readers, making us smile, making us laugh, bewitching us with sentences as light as down." —*Le Monde*

"Rarely has the difficult craft of storytelling been as well mastered." —*Times Literary Supplement*

"A humanist rewriting Foucault with a satirist's wit, Echenoz deftly and amusingly meditates on who we are and what defines us." —*Village Voice*

Ravel

A Novel

Jean Echenoz

Translated from the French
by Linda Coverdale

THE NEW PRESS

NEW YORK
LONDON

This work, published as part of a program providing publication assistance,
received financial support from the Cultural Services of the French Embassy in the United States
and the French American Cultural Exchange.

The New Press also gratefully acknowledges the Florence Gould Foundation
for supporting the publication of this book.

Requests for permission to reproduce selections from this book should be made through our website:
https://thenewpress.com/contact.
Originally published in France by Les Éditions de Minuit,
7, rue Bernard-Palissy, 75006, Paris
Published in the United States by The New Press, New York, 2007
This paperback edition published by The New Press, 2011
Distributed by Two Rivers Distribution

LIBRARY OF CONGRESS CATALOGING-IN-PUBLICATION DATA
Echenoz, Jean.
[Ravel. English]
Ravel : a novel / Jean Echenoz ; translated from the French by Linda Coverdale.
p. cm.
ISBN 978-1-59558-115-0 (hc)
ISBN 978-1-59558-670-4 (pb)
ISBN 978-1-62097-000-3 (e-book)
I. Ravel, Maurice, 1875–1937—Fiction. I. Coverdale, Linda. II. Title.
PQ2665.C5R3813 2007
843'.914—dc22 2006034778

The New Press publishes books that promote and enrich public discussion and understanding of the
issues vital to our democracy and to a more equitable world. These books are made possible by the
enthusiasm of our readers; the support of a committed group of donors, large and small; the collabora-
tion of our many partners in the independent media and the not-for-profit sector; booksellers, who often
hand-sell New Press books; librarians; and above all by our authors.

www.thenewpress.com

Composition by dix!

Printed in the United States of America

JEAN ECHENOZ's *Ravel* is, on the surface, a book that seems to exist largely on the surface. A set of nine intricate, bas-relief cameos etched from the last years of the life of the French composer, it is written with a seemingly dispassionate, detail-obsessed Olympian loft that will recall for some American readers the experiments of the now-old *nouveau roman* with pure description: fiction made without theatrical motive or obvious moralizing. We meet Ravel in his bath and find out all about his bathing, and about his bathtub. We watch him get dressed and are told all about his clothes—the number of suits in his wardrobe, the styles of his cravats, and the color of his shirts. On board the ocean liner *France* on his way to America, we learn all about the luxury liners in their great last days, their fittings and their furnaces; and on a train in America, we learn more than an American reader is ever likely to have known about great American trains.

The "inner life" of Ravel is kept largely at arm's, or finger's, length: glimpses come to us of his struggle to sleep, of his frustrations at bad interpreters—there is a long and very funny section about his composition of the concerto for left hand for Paul Wittgenstein, which the one-armed and humorless pianist then over-elaborates—and of his shock at the success of his deliberately "unmusical" *Boléro*. Yet these are kept as mere mummified glimpses; the life of the book, like the life of the world as Echenoz seems to imagine it, consists less in the heroic struggle of an artistic temperament to assert itself *against* the things of the world than in the gentle, slapstick bumping-intos of minds and passions *with* the things of the world—boats and trains and suits and hotel rooms, and finally, with the exquisitely described surgical sutures that precede the composer's death.

Yet two cheering things soon strike the reader. One is that, while Echenoz is a fanatic miniaturist, he is no minimalist. There is a wonderful (and wonderfully well-researched) generosity in his concentration on worldly surfaces, an appetite to fill in all the blanks around the central figure—a love of facts and functions, of the way things work and sound in all their intractable specificity, that for an American reader will recall to mind Nicholson Baker or the Nabokov of *Pnin*. This expansiveness keeps Echenoz's fictions, for all their haiku-like slenderness, from ever seeming pinched or mean; there is a gentle and understated respect for what in other hands might seem the mere decor and cliché of life, a relish for obvious things that becomes a sober respect for them. And then Echenoz has, despite the evasion of obvious dramatic (or, perhaps he would think, melodramatic) moments, a real gift for human psychology. Echenoz's Ravel is a perfect portrait of the artist-as-an-aging-man, recalling one of Rodin's plasters of the wild-bearded George Bernard Shaw—a thing that touches the edge of cartoon and caricature but is all the more moving for that. The aging artist—overloaded with honors, limited in action, and full of a secret sense of having been, if not misunderstood, then at least more of a failure than the people around him suspect—has never been better drawn. An historical novel in petit point, *Ravel* is also a very large-limbed portrait of an artist approaching death with his own odd kind of confused dignity.

Though Echenoz's material here is historical, rather than contemporary, as in his earlier novels, his small-scale but resonant pictures of near misses and lost men have already made a resonant contribution to contemporary French literature. The historically minded critic might see in Echenoz's diamond-pen-on-glass etchings of a lost time and a now-distant high period of French cultural achievement a sign of the current French cultural predicament, with so much of the good stuff seemingly all behind. A more literary minded American reader might find, in its mix of the pensive and precise, parallels with the work of Donald Bartheleme—and a Francophile reader might find as well echoes of Jacques Tati's style of sober-minded extended comedy, where the dignity of the central figure is all that there is to keep him from the absurd encroachments of the modern world. Whichever reading one chooses to make, Echenoz's work is also a reminder of the still almost inexhaustible resources of the French humanist tradition to make writing come alive through a loving rendition of the skin of things.

Adam Gopnik
April 2007

ONE

LEAVING THE BATHTUB is sometimes quite annoying. First of all, it's a shame to abandon the soapy lukewarm water, where stray hairs wind around bubbles among the scrubbed-off skin cells, for the chill atmosphere of a poorly heated house. Then, if one is the least bit short, and the side of that claw-footed tub the least bit high, it's always a challenge to swing a leg over the edge to feel around, with a hesitant toe, for the slippery tile floor. Caution is advised, to avoid bumping one's crotch or risking a nasty fall. The solution to this predicament would be of course to order a custom-made bathtub, but that entails expenses, perhaps even exceeding the cost of the recently installed but still inadequate central heating. Better to remain submerged up to the neck in the bath for hours, if not forever, using one's right foot to periodically manipulate the hot-water faucet, thus adjusting the thermostat to maintain a comfortable amniotic ambience.

But that cannot last: time presses, as always, and Hélène

Jourdan-Morhange[1] will arrive within the hour. So Ravel climbs out of his bathtub and, when dry, slips into a dressing gown of a refined pearl-gray to clean his teeth with his angle-headed toothbrush; shave without missing one whisker; comb every hair straight back; pluck a stubborn eyebrow bristle that has grown overnight into an antenna. Next, selecting an elegant satin-lined manicure case of finest "lizard-grained" kid from among the hairbrushes, ivory combs, and scent bottles on the dressing table, he takes advantage of the hot water's softening effect on his fingernails to cut them painlessly to the correct length. He glances out the window of the tastefully arranged bathroom: beneath the bare trees, the garden is black and white, the short grass dead, the fountain paralyzed by frost. It is early on one of the last days of 1927. Having slept little and poorly, as he does every night, Ravel is in a bad mood, as he is every morning, without even an inkling of what to wear, which increases his ill humor.

He climbs the stairs of his small, complicated house: three stories, viewed from the garden, but only one is visible from the front. On the third floor, which is level with the street, he examines the latter from a hall window to estimate the number of layers enveloping passers-by, hoping to get some idea of what to put on. But it is much too early for the town of Montfort-l'Amaury. There is nobody and nothing but a little Peugeot 201, all gray and showing its age, already parked in front of his house with Hélène at the wheel. There is nothing else at all to see. A pale sun sits in the overcast sky.

There is nothing to be heard anywhere, either. Silence reigns in the kitchen, Ravel having told Mme. Révelot not to come in while he is away. He is running late as usual, grumbling as he lights a cigarette, forced to dress too quickly at the same time, snatching up whatever clothing comes to hand. Then it's his packing that exasperates him, even though he has only an overnight bag to fill; his squadron of suitcases was transferred to Paris two days ago. Once he is ready, Ravel checks his house, verifying that all the windows are closed, the back door locked, the gas in the kitchen and the electric meter in the front hall turned off. It really is a small place and the inspection doesn't last long, but one can never be too careful. Ravel confirms for the last time that he has indeed turned off the boiler before he leaves, muttering furiously again when he opens the door and icy air suddenly buffets his backswept and still-damp white hair.

So: at the bottom of the flight of eight narrow steps, the 201 sits parked, its brakes gripping the sloping street, with Hélène shivering at the wheel, which she drums on with fingers left bare by her buttercup-yellow knit driving gloves. Hélène is a rather attractive woman who might look somewhat like Orane Demazis,[2] to those who remember that actress, but at that time quite a few women had something of Orane Demazis about them. Hélène has turned up the collar of her skunk-fur coat, beneath which she wears a crêpe dress of a delicate peach color with a vegetal motif and a waistline dropped so low that the bodice seems more like a jacket, while the skirt sports a decorative belt with a horn buckle.

Very pretty. She has been waiting patiently. For what is beginning to feel like a long time.

For more than half an hour, on this frigid morning between two holidays, Hélène has been waiting for Ravel, who appears at last, carrying his overnight case. As for his ensemble, he is wearing a slate-gray suit beneath his short, chocolate-brown overcoat: not bad either, although old-fashioned and perhaps a touch lightweight for the season. Cane hooked over his forearm, gloves folded back at the wrist, he looks like a stylish punter or even an owner in the stands for the running of the Prix de Diane or the weighing-in at Enghien, but a breeder less interested in his yearling than in dissociating himself from the classic gray cutaways or linen blazers. He climbs briskly into the Peugeot, sits back with a sigh and, pinching the pleats of his trousers at the knees, tugs gently to keep them from bagging. Well, he says, undoing the top button of his overcoat, I believe we can get going. Turned toward him, Hélène swiftly inspects Ravel from head to toe: his lisle socks and silk pocket handkerchief, as always, nicely match his tie.

You might perhaps have had me wait in your house rather than in the car, she ventures, starting the engine. You could see how cold it is. With quite a dry smile, Ravel points out that he had to do a little straightening up before his departure, it was quite a chore, he was dashing all over. On top of not getting a wink of sleep, as usual, he also had to rise at dawn and he hates that, she knows how he hates that. And besides she knows perfectly well how tiny his place is, they would have been in each other's way. All the same, observes Hélène, you've made me catch my death. Nonsense, Hélène, he says, lighting a Gauloise. Really . . . And when does it leave, exactly, this train?

Twelve past eleven, replies Hélène, letting in the clutch, and in next to no time they drive across a Montfort-l'Amaury as frozen and deserted as an ice floe in the steely light. Near the church, before they leave Montfort, they pass in front of a large bourgeois mansion where the yellow rectangle of one upstairs window leads Ravel to remark that his friend Zogheb[3] seems to be already awake, after which they press on to Versailles, where they take the Avenue de Paris. When Hélène hesitates at an intersection, letting the car drift for a moment, Ravel frets briefly. But you're such a bad driver! he exclaims. My brother Édouard is much better at this. I don't think you'll ever get there. As they approach Sèvres, Hélène again brakes suddenly when she spots a man on the sidewalk wearing a felt hat and carrying under one arm what looks like a large painting tied up in newspaper. Since the man seems to be waiting, she stops to let him cross but above all to study Ravel, whose face is more lean, pale, and drawn than ever: when he closes his eyes for a second, he resembles his own death mask. Aren't you feeling well?

He says that he's all right, that he should be fine but that he still feels quite run-down. After ordering a battery of tests for him, his doctor, upset by Ravel's refusal of the prescribed year of complete rest, wanted to put him on stimulants to prepare him for this trip. Which meant that he had to undergo massive injections of cytoserum, natrum cacodylate, and extracts of pituitary and adrenal glands—it was one shot after another, not much fun. And in spite of everything he's still not really feeling like his old self. When Hélène suggests that he change treatments, he replies that a colleague has just written him with the same advice, urging him to try homeopathy: some people simply swear by it, homeopathy. Well, fine, he'll look into it when he returns. Then he falls silent to watch Sèvres slip past for a moment but in fact there's nothing much to see this morning in Sèvres either, except gray locked-up buildings, black shut-up cars, dark buttoned-up clothing, somber hunched-up shoulders. He's not all that sure anymore that he feels like leaving, now. It's always the same story, isn't it: he accepts these offers without thinking about them and at the last moment they drive him to despair. And what about the cigarettes—is Hélène quite certain that his cigarettes will be delivered to him throughout the trip? Hélène replies that it has all been arranged. And the tickets? She does have the tickets? Everything is here, says Hélène, pointing to her purse.

They enter Paris by the Porte de Saint-Cloud, find the Seine, and follow its embankments to Concorde, where they turn north to speed through the city toward the Gare Saint-Lazare. Things are livelier than in the western suburbs, obviously, but not really by much. They see men on bicycles, women without hats, posters on walls, quite a few automobiles, including the occasional luxury model from Panhard-Levasseur or Rosengart. Coming to the end of the Rue de la Pépinière, for example, they notice, heading down the Rue de Rome, a long, two-toned Salmson VAL3, as sleek as a pimp's pumps.

Shortly before ten o'clock, Hélène parks her humble Peugeot in front of the Hôtel Terminus, whence they proceed to the Criterion, a bar on the Cour du Havre where Ravel is a regular and two singers of the kind known in those days as *chanteuses intelligentes,* Marcelle Gérar and Madeleine Grey,[4] are waiting patiently with their hot drinks. Ravel takes his sweet time ordering a coffee, then another that he drinks even more slowly while the three young women, exchanging questioning looks, consult the clock on the wall with increasing frequency. Growing worried, they finally move things along, escorting Ravel resolutely across the street to the station, which they enter a good half-hour before the departure of the train. The special isn't even at the platform when they arrive, Ravel leading the way, trailed by his friends who are helping, more or less, two porters from the Terminus drag along his four bulky suitcases plus a trunk. This luggage is quite heavy, but these young women are so very fond of music.

Leaning out over the tracks, Ravel lights a Gauloise before pulling from his overcoat pocket a copy of *L'Intransigeant,* which he has just bought at a kiosk after failing to find his customary *Le Populaire.* Since the year is almost over, the newspaper sums it up in time-honored fashion, recalling the reestablishment of constituency polls, the launching of the ocean liner *Cap Arcona,*[5] the electrocution of Sacco and Vanzetti, the production of the first talking picture, and the invention of television. Although unable to include everything that has happened worldwide this year in the field of music (the birth of Gerry Mulligan,[6] for example), *L'Intransigeant* does mention the recent inauguration of the concert hall Salle Pleyel, over which Ravel lingers, seeking and finding his name, then shrugs his shoulders. When the breathless young women rejoin him, leaving the factotums of the Terminus to pile the baggage into a pyramidion on the edge of the platform, Hélène inquires timidly about the latest news, gesturing toward the paper. Nothing much, he replies, nothing much. In any case, it's a right-wing paper, isn't it.

The special arrives at last, hauled by a type 120 locomotive, a hybrid version of the high-speed III Buddicom. The porters begin stowing the luggage in the baggage compartments while Ravel takes his leave of the ladies, deploying his very best manners: compliments and hand-kisses, thanks and professions of friendship. Then he gets on the train and easily finds his reserved seat in the first-class car, by the window, which he lowers. They engage in more smiling and ever-smaller small talk until departure time, when the ladies pluck from their purses handkerchiefs they then begin to wave. Ravel waves nothing, contenting himself with one last wry smile and an uplifted hand before closing the window and returning to his paper.

He is leaving for the harbor station at Le Havre to sail to North America. It is his first trip there; it will be his last. He now has ten years, on the nose, left to live.

TWO

As for the ocean liner *France*, second of that name, aboard which Ravel will head off to America, she still has nine active years ahead of her before her sale to the Japanese for scrap. Flagship of the transatlantic fleet, a mass of riveted steel capped with four smokestacks (one a dummy), she is a block 723 feet long and 75 feet wide, sent into service twenty-five years ago from the Ateliers de Saint-Nazaire-Penhoët. From first to fourth class, the vessel can carry some two thousand passengers besides her five hundred crewmen and officers. This ship of 22,500 tons burden—propelled at a cruising speed of twenty-three knots by four groups of Parsons turbines fed by thirty-two Prudhon-Capus boilers generating forty thousand units of horsepower—needs only six days for a smooth transatlantic voyage, while the fleet's other steamers, less powerfully driven, take nine to huff and puff across.

A Ritz or Plaza under steam, the *France* triumphs not only in speed but in comfort as well: Ravel has barely stepped on board when a band of impeccable cabin boys in brand-new red livery leads him along stairs and passageways to his reserved suite. It's a luxurious apartment with chintz curtains, inlaid woodwork of sycamore, Hungarian oak, kingwood, and bird's-eye maple, furniture of citron wood and palisander, and a spacious bathroom of vermeil and clouded marble. After rapidly inspecting the premises, Ravel glances out one of the portholes that still, for the time being, overlook the quay: he observes the throng of well-wishers jostling one another while waving handkerchiefs—as at Saint-Lazare—but hats and flowers as well and other things besides. He doesn't try to recognize anyone in that crowd; although he welcomed an escort to the train station, he prefers to set sail on his own. After he has taken off his coat, unpacked three items, and arranged his toilet articles around the sinks, Ravel goes off to reserve a seat in the dining room from the maître d', then a steamer chair from the deck steward. Waiting for the ship to get under way, Ravel spends a few moments in the nearest smoking lounge, where the mahogany walls are inlaid with mother-of-pearl. There he has one or two more Gauloises and—judging from certain lingering or averted looks, certain discreet or knowing smiles—the impression that people have recognized him.

That's not unusual, and with good reason: fifty-two years old, he is at the height of his fame, Stravinsky his only rival as the world's most revered musician, and Ravel's picture is often in the papers. That isn't unusual, either, given his appearance: his lean, close-shaven face and long narrow nose form two triangles set perpendicularly to each other. Dark eyes, a restless and piercing gaze, bushy eyebrows, hair slicked back to reveal a high forehead, thin lips, prominent ears without lobes, a matte complexion. Elegantly aloof, icily polite, not particularly talkative, he is a man of courteous simplicity, gaunt but jaunty, dressed to the nines at all times.

He was not always so clean-shaven, however. In his youth he tried everything: sideburns at twenty-five, with a monocle and chatelaine, then a pointed beard at thirty followed by a squared beard and, later, a trial run with a mustache. At thirty-five he shaved all that off, at the same time taming his mane, which went from bouffant to permanently severe and sleek and quickly white. But his chief characteristic is his shortness, which pains him and makes his head seem a little too large for his body. Five feet three inches; ninety-nine pounds; thirty inches around the chest. Ravel has the build of a jockey and thus of William Faulkner who, at the time, is dividing his life between two cities (Oxford, Mississippi, and New Orleans), two books (*Mosquitoes* and *Sartoris*), and two whiskeys (Jack Daniel's and Jack Daniel's).

A blurry sun sits in the cloudy sky when Ravel, alerted by the sirens announcing that the anchor is weighed, goes to the veranda deck of the liner to observe the activity from inside the enclosed promenade. The deep fatigue of which he complained that morning in the Peugeot seems to vanish at the song of the three-ton sirens: suddenly he feels light, enthusiastic, charged with enough energy to go out into the fresh air. But that doesn't last: very soon he feels very cold without his overcoat, pulls his jacket tightly closed across his chest, and shivers. The wind has come up suddenly, clamping his clothes against his skin, denying their existence and function, attacking the surface of his body head-on, so that the man feels naked and must try repeatedly to light a cigarette, since the matches haven't time to catch fire. He finally succeeds but then it's the Gauloise, which, as in the mountains (brief memory of the sanatorium), no longer tastes right: the wind is taking advantage of the smoke to slip alongside it into Ravel's lungs, now chilling his body from the inside, assailing him from all directions, taking his breath away, mussing his hair, sending cigarette ash into his eyes and onto his clothes—he's overmatched, best beat a retreat. He returns with everyone else to the shelter of the glass wall to observe the steamship's maneuvers as she turns heavily in the harbor, crosses the roads, bellowing as she goes, and emerges grandly off Sainte-Adresse and the Cap de la Hève.

Since they are swiftly out at sea, the passengers have just as swiftly lost interest in the view. One after another has deserted the enclosure to go marvel at the sumptuous fittings of the *France,* her bronzes and rosewood, gilt and damask, carpets and candelabras. Ravel remains, preferring to contemplate as long as possible the green-and-gray surface streaked fleetingly with white, which might furnish him with a melodic line, a rhythm, a leitmotif, who knows. He's well aware that it never works that way, that inspiration does not exist, that composition takes place only at the keys. Still, since this is the first time he has ever seen such a spectacle, it doesn't hurt to try. After a moment, however, it seems that no motif has presented itself and that Ravel, too, is growing bored: the shadow of tedium has its foot in the door, hand in hand with the boomerang return of fatigue—which incoherent reflections provide more proof that it wouldn't be a bad idea to rest awhile. Ravel wanders in the bowels of the ship looking for his suite, almost amused to be lost in that apartment house on the high seas. Back in his quarters, he lies down on the bed to wait for Southampton, where the *France* will put in only briefly toward sunset. After which, the Atlantic crossing will truly begin.

Once more he feels weak, having breakfasted barely at all on a hard-boiled egg he downed on the quay, and besides, the huge volume of sea air has saturated his frail chest. Stretched out, he tries to nap for a moment, but since his nervous tension is at war with his weakness, this conflict merely goads both increasingly exasperated contenders into engendering a third malaise that is mental and physical and greater than the sum of its parts. Although Ravel sits up and attempts to read, his eyes skid over the lines without grasping the slightest meaning. He gives in and gets up, pacing the suite, studying it in detail without any better result, and finally decides to rummage through his suitcases to make sure he hasn't forgotten anything. No, not a thing. In addition to a small blue valise crammed full of Gauloises, the other bags contain—among other things—sixty shirts, twenty pairs of shoes, seventy-five ties, and twenty-five sets of pajamas that, given the principle of the part for the whole, offer some idea of the scope of his wardrobe.

He has always taken care with the selection, maintenance, and replacement of his clothes. When not following the latest fashions, he invariably precedes them: he was the first in France to wear pastel shirts, the first to dress entirely in white if he so chose (pullover, trousers, socks, shoes), and he has always been most attentive and particular on this point. In his youth he was observed wearing formal black with a stunning vest, a jabot at his neck, an opera hat, and butter-yellow gloves. He was observed with Satie in a raglan overcoat and bowler hat, carrying a Malacca cane with a curved handle (this was before Satie began badmouthing him). He was observed gazing into the distance, one hand tucked inside the front of a frock coat, and this time sporting a cronstadt hat, during a candidates' recess at the Prix de Rome[7] competition—this was before he'd failed the examination five times in a row, having taken too many liberties with the assigned cantatas for the jury members not to have taken umbrage, declaring that although Ravel had the right to consider them fuddy-duddies, he would not get away with treating them as idiots. He was observed in a black-and-white suit, black-and-white-striped socks, white shoes, and a straw hat, his arm still prolonged by his cane, the cane being to the hand what a smile is to the lips. He was observed as well, chez Alma Mahler, upholstered in a striking taffeta—this was also before Alma let some ambiguous gossip about him flourish unchecked.

Apart from all that, he owns a black dressing gown embroidered in gold and two tuxedos, one in Paris, the other in Montfort.

When, announcing Southampton, the sirens raise their voices once again, Ravel dons his overcoat to go watch the ship draw alongside the quay. Viewed from the upper deck in the abruptly fallen darkness, the port is much better illuminated once the yellowy spangles of the street lamps have outlined both banks of the channel leading into the harbor. Ravel begins to discern the frames of the tall cranes looming over the piers, a *Mauretania* in dry dock, the bronze angel towering atop the *Titanic* memorial, and a green train of the Southern Railway sitting alongside the quay on which, shortly before the steamship berths, Ravel also notices a small group of people. When the vessel has been made fast, one of them steps forward, folder in hand, and climbs briskly on board as soon as the gangway has been secured.

Gentle voice, sage expression, sober dress, wing collar, monocle: Georges Jean-Aubry seems like a professor or a lawyer or a doctor, or else a professor of legal medicine. Ravel met him more than thirty years ago, Salle Érard, at the premiere of his *Miroirs* performed by Ricardo Viñes. Jean-Aubry, who lives in London, has traveled to Southampton to greet Ravel during this brief stopover and present him with a copy of *La Flèche d'or*, his just-completed translation of Joseph Conrad's *The Arrow of Gold*, to be published in the coming year by Gallimard. Convenient reading material, he thinks, for Ravel during the voyage. As for Conrad, he has been dead for three years.

THREE

THREE YEARS BEFORE CONRAD DIED, Ravel and Jean-Aubry had gone to see him. The visit had been no picnic. More solidly built than Ravel, Conrad was, like him, a short man of angular features and rather few words. And even less inclined to pour out his feelings, given his ill health, neurasthenia, and erratic moods, his wrists and fingers crippled with gout and lumbago. When he was willing to talk, it was in colorful French with a Marseilles accent, a souvenir of his first stay in France: three years aboard various vessels of the Compagnie Delestang & Fils, as a passenger at first, then an apprentice in the merchant marine, then a steward, before his attempt to kill himself—when he aimed to put a bullet through his heart but missed, right after Ravel was born.

So, Ravel often proving, like Conrad, not too chatty, their conversation had had a tendency to dry up, despite a few oases where the former spoke guardedly of his enjoyment of the latter's writing, while the latter strove tactfully to hide his ignorance of the former's music. In this desert, Jean-Aubry had shuttled between the two mutes like an exhausted fireman, trying to bestow upon each one in turn a little artificial respiration. On the deck of the *France*, that meeting evokes a few brief memories, and after Jean-Aubry promises to send Ravel a copy of *Frère-de-la-côte*, his translation of Conrad's *The Rover*, also recently completed and due to appear at the same time as *La Flèche d'or*, the sirens bring that conversation to an end and it's adieu Southampton.

Back in his suite, Ravel doesn't feel up to changing for dinner. All things considered, tired as he is, this evening he doesn't really feel like facing the dining room, either. Informing the staff of this after having room service bring him a Pernod, he prefers to compose his menu himself, finding it amusing to reproduce his daily terrestrial fare in Montfort-l'Amaury out on the high seas: mackerel *au vinaigre*, a thick steak (*bleu*), some gruyère, fruit in season, and a carafe of white wine to wash everything down.

Then it's still early, not even nine-thirty once all that has been eaten. After dinner at Montfort, ordinarily, since sleep is inconceivable, the night has barely begun. The reduced scale of Ravel's home condenses a wealth of possible activities, even though they may be only momentary, or merely idle impulses. From the kitchen to the drawing room, via the library and the piano, a last little turn around the garden—Ravel can have lots to do even though he doesn't do a thing, until he must finally head off to bed after all. But here? No distractions, no tasks, no attachments, no desire, either, to go kill time in the bars or the gaming rooms of the *France*. Although his suite is of course smaller than the house in Montfort, it produces a doubly inverse effect: too roomy in one sense, at the same time it allots his body the precise range allowed by a hospital room—a vital but atrophied space with nothing to cling to but oneself, and which still feels like a floating sanatorium. Ravel turns to the first page of Jean-Aubry's Conrad translation and considers the first sentence: *The pages which follow have been extracted from a pile of manuscript which was apparently meant for the eye of one woman only*—not a bad start but this evening no, not in the mood. Once won't matter, why doesn't he just go to bed.

So here he is undressing. Then, after hesitating over his pajamas—in the green spectrum—and finally opting for the emerald instead of the veronese, he unfolds one of his twenty-five suits of sleepwear. So doing, he yawns and feels drowsy, which comforts him in his decision. He turns off every light except the bedside lamp, intending after all to read awhile before trying to sleep. Once in bed, he opens the translation again, tackling the second sentence and pressing on: *She seems to have been the writer's childhood's friend. They had parted as children, or very little more than children. Years passed*, his eyes are already blinking by the end of the fourth sentence, he has completely lost track, he'll try again tomorrow. Reaching confidently for the lamp, as if they were old friends, Ravel turns out the light, and at barely ten o'clock, drops off—he who invariably chases sleep until dawn only to snag just some mediocre cut-rate, secondhand variety or indeed none at all—like a rock down a well.

He sleeps and the next day, as on each day from time imme-
morial on the ocean liners of the world, everyone is served a cup
of bouillon at eleven o'clock out on deck. Wrapped in a thick
plaid blanket on a deck chair, nice and warm despite the salt
spray, you sip the steaming bouillon while contemplating the
ocean; it's quite pleasant. Deck chairs like these, soon to appear in
gardens and on beaches, on terraces and balconies, are currently
to be found only on the decks of transatlantic liners, which ap-
pellation they will keep, out of attachment, when they set foot
ashore.

Ravel's chair has blue and white stripes, and the promenade
deck, made of yellow pine from the Canary Islands, is veined
with red. So: Ravel is gazing at the ocean like the other passengers
without striking up a relationship with them, that's not in his na-
ture. Although he has given up the cold aloofness of his youth, he
has hardly become a man who throws his arms around other people. To his right is a couple who look like industrialists; to the
left, a woman of thirty-five completely on her own, her eyes moving back and forth between oceanic contemplation and the reading of a book that almost causes Ravel, who is trying to decipher
its title, to discreetly dislocate his neck.

As for him, open upon his knees lies the manuscript left by
Jean-Aubry, introduced by the author as "A Story Between Two
Notes." Ravel has just finished reading the first one—*A remarkable
instance of the great power of mere individuality over the young*—and now,
his bouillon finished, since the air is growing chilly, he abandons

the deck for the reading room, pausing along the way to examine the décor of the grand staircase of yellow and gray Lunel marble, a replica of the one in the mansion of the Comte de Toulouse in Rambouillet. While the other passengers scatter, some toward the gymnasium or the squash court, others toward the pool, the electric Turkish baths, or the miniature golf course, perhaps the boat deck for a game of shuffleboard, or the smoking room to be fleeced by professional cheats, Ravel prefers to continue reading while awaiting lunchtime. When the moment arrives, however, rather than proceed to the dining room where he has a reserved seat, he elects to postpone the meal, which he'll eat a little later at the à la carte restaurant. Fewer restrictions there: one goes when one likes and eats what one likes. As it is the last day of the year, the evening threatens to be long, lively, bountiful, noisy—in the expectation of which, Ravel prefers to eat lightly.

The afternoon begins at the movie theater, with *Napoléon,* which along with *Metropolis* has just tolled the knell for silent films. Ravel watches *Napoléon* for the second time without displeasure, although a fondness for light humor and his penchant for laughing at trifles would have led him to prefer less serious recent works such as *The Madonna of the Sleeping Cars,* which he'd found quite amusing last year, or even *Patouillard and His Cow* or indeed *Bigorno the Roofer.* Then, after a little lie-down in his suite, he prepares, donning tuxedo number one, to go have dinner, in the first-class dining room this time. He can't get out of that, unavoidably at the captain's table, the latter sporting his inevitable short white beard and dress whites. And during this dinner, no less inexorably, given the imminence of the tenth anniversary of the armistice, the conversation will turn to the Great War, with everyone contributing a modest memory. Since Ravel finds himself seated near the industrial couple noticed this morning out on deck, they are the ones who hear about his private war.

In '14 he had honestly tried to enlist, even though the authorities had exempted him from every kind of military obligation, explaining bluntly that he was too frail. Home again disappointed, then convinced he'd hit upon a persuasive idea (because he ardently wanted to become, go figure, a bombardier), he'd gone back to insist to the recruiters that it was precisely his light weight that fitted him for aviation. Although that seemed logical, his argument hadn't swayed them, they'd wanted nothing to do with it. Too light, they kept saying, too light, you're at least four and a half pounds underweight. Since he kept at them relentlessly, though, after eight months under siege they had finally accepted him, rolling their eyes heavenward with a shrug and finding nothing better to do than assign him with a straight face to the motor transport service as a driver, heavy-vehicle section, of course. That's how an enormous military truck came to drive one day down the Champs-Élysées containing a small figure in a too-large blue greatcoat clinging to the too-big steering wheel for dear life, a wharf rat riding an elephant.

He had been posted at first to the garage on the Rue de Vaugirard, then sent in March of '16 to the front, not far from

Verdun, still assigned to drive heavy vehicles. Now a full-fledged soldier, a gas-masked, helmeted, goatskin-clad *poilu*, he had driven several times through artillery barrages so fierce one would have thought that a faction of music-hating enemy gunners had singled him out, perhaps even had it in for him personally. It seems that no one in any motor service, even the ambulance corps, could have been more at risk than Ravel had been in the 75 section: 75mm guns, mind you, mounted on armored trucks. One day, his vehicle broke down and he found himself on his own out in open country, where he spent a week alone à la Crusoe. Taking advantage of the situation, he transcribed a few songs from the local birds, which, weary of the war, had finally decided to ignore it, to no longer interrupt their trills at the slightest blast or take offense at the constant rumbling of nearby explosions.

This tale having met with much success at the dinner table, we may take a moment to consider the festive repast itself, a quite commonplace gala menu: caviar, lobster, quail from Egypt, plovers' eggs, hothouse grapes, all sluiced down with everything imaginable. Once the meal has been dispatched and it's time for liqueurs, the captain sends a subtle smile Ravel's way while briefly waving two fingers, at which signal a couple of musicians suddenly appear in tails and boiled shirts: one carries a violin, and the other takes his seat at the piano, the cue for silence to fall throughout the dining room.

After glancing and nodding at one another, they attack the first movement of the sonata Ravel completed that year, dedicated to Hélène, and premiered himself with Enesco on violin, Salle Érard again, in May. Ravel is embarrassed, to say the least; almost a little annoyed. At a concert, he usually steps out for a cigarette when one of his pieces is played. He doesn't like to be there during the performance. But he can't possibly slip away—they meant well by offering him this little surprise—and tries to smile while seething inside. Particularly since they're not doing too well with it, his new sonata, he finds. And when after a good fifteen minutes they wind up the last movement, *Perpetuum mobile,* another problem arises: applaud or not? Because applauding one's own work is as disagreeable as not applauding the performers. In his uncertainty he stands up, obviously reaching out toward the two hired musicians as he claps his hands, then he warmly shakes theirs, and joins them in acknowledging the cheers of the entire first class of the *France.*

After dinner, after the traditional collection on behalf of the Seafarers Charity, after Ravel has contributed as he always does, the party can begin. This considerable celebration unfolds throughout the ship's upper decks until late at night or even into the morning for some souls, once the revelers have congratulated one another at length upon the stroke of midnight to salute the new year, greetings which—given the varied geographical origins of the passengers, the time lag, and the alcohol-fueled enthusiasm—ring out hourly in ever-jollier fashion until the first rays of dawn. Balloons, confetti, garlands, and streamers are everywhere you look in the lounges, smoking rooms, cafés, verandas, and passageways enlivened at every turn by different kinds of orchestras ready to satisfy any sort of taste. A chamber group plays soberly at a respectful distance from a dance band, while a French cabaret singer fraternizes with a Russian quartet, but Ravel, for his part, spends most of his night among the drunken Americans not far from a jazz combo, attentive to this new and perishable art.

FOUR

THE NEXT MORNING he arises late, having lain in bed so long that he misses the bouillon on deck. Then, clad in casual seersucker, he takes a stroll around the more or less deserted promenade deck, where two cabin boys with trays are collecting the bowls scattered among the feet of the canvas chairs. The sea is an almost-black green.

Time, aboard ship, can very quickly hang heavily. What's more, the days, one soon finds, not only seem longer than on land— they really are: thanks to the division of the time difference during the crossing, they easily last their twenty-five hours. However, the tameness of the entertainment on offer also helps stretch out these shipboard days. Because the truth is, in first class, passengers spend most of their time changing clothes thrice daily, it's their chief recreation. Aside from that, the weaker sex lounges a great deal in deck chairs beneath a glass roof, while the stronger one plays quite a lot of cards—whist, bridge, poker—as well as

checkers, chess, and dominoes. A few parlor games are also organized, including wooden-horse races that support a pari-mutuel,
while hefty sums are also wagered each evening (save on Sunday,
for propriety's sake) on the precise position of the ship. But luckily for Ravel, who is a good swimmer, there is a pool, upon
emerging from which he immerses himself every day, in the bar-
ber shop, in a complete reading of *L'Atlantique*, the ship's daily
paper printed up from news received by wireless from radio sta-
tions ashore.

Exploring the vessel is another possibility. Although passengers in first class are kept separate from those in lower classes,
where the atmosphere is more informal, the ship is vast enough
for such a visit to take up an entire day. Ravel doesn't pass up such
an opportunity, striding around the decks, lingering on the
bridge near the officers' quarters, spending a moment in the wireless room and then the chart house, where he asks questions
about all the equipment, and then it's down to admire the turbines in the engine room, a monstrous stomach where the heat
and din give a good idea of hell, but he has always liked machines
and factories, foundries and red-hot steel—wheels are better
than waves at suggesting rhythms to him. Afterward he can return
to the comforts of the upper decks, continue his reading on the
café terrace, loiter near the gymnasium or look in on the tennis
court up on the sun deck. Just once, because he's not very reli-
gious, he visits the chapel, which as we know is traditionally the

first place fitted out when a steamship is built and the last to be used in case of misfortune.

Fine, but all that only gets us so far, and since all the days are alike, why go on about it, let's skip over the next three. Two days before the *France* arrives in New York, Ravel gives a little concert that evening by popular demand. For this performance of short pieces, he has rejected the pianist's uniform of black tails in favor of more relaxed, or even slightly facetious attire. It's in striped shirt, checked suit, and red tie that he plays his *Prélude*, composed fifteen years ago now, and then, accompanied by a laboring hireling, his first sonata for piano and violin, from thirty years ago. With his knees barely tucked under the keyboard, which his hands do not dominate but hover above, palms flat as if approaching from a low angle, he runs his too-short, gnarled, somewhat squared-off fingers over the keys. While unsuited for octave reaches, his fingers feature exceptionally powerful thumbs, the thumbs of a strangler, easily dislocated and set high on the palm, quite far from the rest of the hand and almost as long as the indexes. His hands are not really those of a pianist and besides, he doesn't have a great technique. It's easy to see that he isn't experienced: he plays stiffly, with lots of mistakes.

That he's so clumsy at the piano is also due to the laziness he has never shaken off since childhood; being so light, he has no desire to tire himself out on such a heavy instrument. He's well aware that performing a piece, especially a slow one, demands a physical effort he'd rather not have to make. So breeziness is better, which he has recently pushed to the point of composing the accompaniment of *Ronsard à son âme*[8] for the left hand alone, having planned on smoking with his right. In short he plays badly but, well, he plays. He is, he knows, the opposite of a virtuoso but, since no one understands anything about it, he pulls through perfectly.

The day before their arrival, shortly before teatime, the captain knocks on the door of his suite. Wearing a smoking jacket with a floral pattern, Ravel opens the door to his visitor who, bowing slightly, carries under his left arm a thick, gilt-edged volume bound in dark-red leather. Ravel knows immediately what's up: the ship's visitors' book, in which the captain asks him not without ceremony to inscribe a few words. He replies but of course.

After placing the volume on a pedestal table, the captain opens it with care and respectfully leafs through it to the first available blank page, which he shows to Ravel. To give himself time to come up with something appropriate, the latter looks back through the preceding pages, which are well stocked, the *France* having been in active service since her delivery date in April 1912, with hundreds of tributes set above names that Ravel more or less recognizes from the most prominent ranks of French society: politics, industry, finance, the clergy, arts and letters, official circles. He examines the object with apparent curiosity but mostly, having no idea what to inscribe inside it, in order to search rapidly through the handwritten compliments for one that might inspire him.

Thus employed, he is struck as always by the diversity of the signatures. Had he the time, Ravel would amuse himself by trying to deduce the personalities of the writers from their graphic styles, along the line originally laid down by Baldi and developed by the Abbé Michon, Crépieux-Jamin, and others. Thus, certain signers merely write their first and last names, simply and legibly, underlined or not, said underscoring being occasionally independent of the name, sometimes linked to it by an extension of its last letter. Through a scruple of modesty, an access of artlessness (unless an excess of pride), their initials may not even be written in capitals. Easily deciphered, such signatures are nevertheless in the minority. Most of the others are more or less complicated and successful stylizations of a surname, the authors having a grand old time as if they'd seen a chance at last, for once in their lives, to play the artist. Usually dissuasive of all hope of legibility, these signatures consist of interminable flourishes ornamented with loops, arabesques, spirals, up-and-down strokes, swooping off in all directions like dead-drunk ice-skaters, enhanced by mysterious dots and lines, so sophisticated that it's impossible not only to puzzle out the names these signatures supposedly embody but sometimes even to determine in which direction they were inscribed, with which movement the author began this graphic undertaking. When the signature is just too difficult to decode, a respectful hand has penciled in beneath it the identity of its creator.

Whatever the solution adopted for these signatures, what Ravel concludes above all is that the whole business must take an outlandish amount of time to draw. For his part he merely pens a rapid and temperate tribute in his tall, nervous handwriting, all in peaks, followed by his perfectly legible and not even underlined first and last names, barely ornamented with the prolonged vertical down-strokes of their capital letters.

After the captain has left, Ravel takes advantage of the pen still in his hand to write some friends a few short, rather conventional letters, without taking too much trouble over them. In one, addressed to the Delages, he allows as how he hasn't misused his deluxe suite much by working. In another, intended for Roland-Manuel,[9] he supposes that no one has probably ever had a more pleasant crossing at this time of year. Another note for Hélène, one for Édouard, and there, that's done. He changes clothes once more before sealing these messages into their envelopes to drop them off at the Information Desk, where mail is collected to be flown out by a seaplane catapulted from the ship's after deck. Then, since the voyage is drawing to a close, it's a good time to pack the luggage before filling out the customs declarations.

And that evening, at dinner, everybody will behave as usual in such situations: addresses exchanged, plans to meet again, repeated toasts. After which everyone will go off to bed, except for those who will prefer to stay up as late as possible in the bar and go out on deck at dawn, to breathe in the first scents of the American mainland, and soon contemplate the embarkation of the harbor pilot at Ambrose Light before the Statue of Liberty is sighted and the ship begins moving up the Hudson. Meanwhile, reclaimed by insomnia, Ravel has just shut the translation of *The Arrow of Gold* after rereading the last line two or three times: *But what else could he have done with it?*

FIVE

In New York, on the morning of the fourth, a welcoming committee awaits Ravel on the pier. A frigid sun sits in the clear sky. There are various delegates from musical societies, presidents of associations, two municipal representatives, a swarm of press photographers brandishing huge flash cameras, editorial cartoonists, cameramen, and reporters with notebooks, press cards tucked into their hatbands. Up on the bridge, at first Ravel cannot identify anyone in that throng, but he soon catches sight of Schmitz,[10] who played his *Trio* ten years ago (that was when he'd met Hélène), Schmitz who has graciously organized this entire American tour. And since he then recognizes Bolette Natanson,[11] not far from Schmitz, Ravel smiles broadly at them, waves his hand, then leans out over the guardrail, unable to contain himself any longer: Wait till you see, he shouts to them, the splendid ties I brought with me!

As soon as Ravel has disembarked from the *France,* people

crowd around him, watched enviously by the other first-class passengers for whom only their families, at best, are waiting. He is greeted with handshakes he finds a bit too familiar and three short speeches of which he understands not a word, having no ear for any foreign language except Basque. While he is barely able to ask for directions in English, he never understands the replies in any case, but from now on that situation will not apply since he isn't on his own: during the next four months he will never be on his own, in fact sometimes he will not be enough on his own. Now he is being escorted to a long black Pierce-Arrow convertible unlike anything he's ever seen in the movies and is soon whisked off to the Langdon Hotel, to his reserved suite on the eighth floor.

Flanked by his manager and the first violinist of the Boston Symphony Orchestra, who is acting as an interpreter, he spends this first day giving interviews and meeting various people while baskets of fruit and flowers stream into the Langdon, so many bouquets piling up that the hotel runs out of vases. Ravel spends much of the next four days in taxis speeding to all sorts of appointments, rehearsals, invitations, and receptions—including one particularly grueling affair given by the wife of the inventor Edison, where three hundred strangers approach one after the other to speak English to him. The concert in New York is an apotheosis: three thousand five hundred people give him a standing ovation for half an hour, throwing him kisses and armfuls of new flowers, bringing the house down with shouting and whistling the way they do in this country when they're really pleased, until he's compelled to go onstage which as a rule he doesn't much like. And quite late in the evenings, after the round of dance halls, giant movie houses, and Harlem revues, Ravel returns to the Langdon exhausted.

Then it's off across the United States. After the concert in Cambridge followed by a reception, still in his tuxedo he must dash to catch the train to Boston—he stays at the Copley Plaza—where he triumphs again in concert, another three hundred hands to shake, everyone assuring him constantly that they love him and sometimes that he seems English before dragging him off to nightclubs or shadow plays. Same thing back in New York, Carnegie Hall, and afterward always social events in his honor with Bartók, Varèse, Gershwin, in the Madison Avenue homes of chic people who persist in asking him, of course, to play something for us. So he plays; he will have to play constantly, in the concert halls and at private parties where not without some trepidation he will occasionally have to conduct as well—from now on it won't ever stop.

Same welcome in Chicago blanketed by snow, except that at the last moment Ravel refuses to play. Unable to find the suitcase containing his patent-leather shoes, he refuses to appear without them—street shoes with a conductor's tails are out of the question—until a singer races in a taxi to the station to fetch his suitcase from the cloakroom. They begin thirty minutes late but no matter: a new ovation followed by fanfare served up by the orchestra's brass section when he returns to bow at the end of the concert. Same welcome in Cleveland, new fanfare with three thousand five hundred new people on their feet, same excellent welcome everywhere, things look rather promising. Just one little problem: the food is bad. So bad that in Chicago, invited to dinner at a millionaire's house, Ravel cuts the evening short to hurry to the hotel, in the harsh cold and proverbial wind, so that he can send down for a steak. Just one more little problem: it's impossible to sleep. Given the life they've got him leading, only on the train can he get a little rest, if any.

Luckily there is no shortage of trains, and luckily as well it's aboard luxurious convoys that he must crisscross the North American continent in all directions, because the itinerary they've set up for him is aberrant. It's a route as disconcerting as a fly's through the air and will have him make, in climates glacial to tropical, absurd round trips, dubious stopovers, and ill-chosen byways on a tour of twenty-five cities.

The trains, named *Zephyr, Hiawatha, Empire State Express, Sunset Limited,* or *Santa Fe de Luxe,* carry on in their own way the standard of comfort maintained aboard the *France.* As refined as an ocean liner, they are sumptuous five-star hotels made up of fifteen eighty-ton cars, and the brow of each streamlined locomotive, with the profile of a rocket, is equipped with a colossal central headlight. The cars offer every imaginable service: desks for businessmen, movies, dancing, manicure and hairdressing salons, consultations with beauticians, a concert hall with an organ for

Sunday services, a library, and numerous bars. As for the state-
rooms with all their precious woods, carpets, leaded-glass windows, and drapes, they are furnished with canopied four-poster
beds and bathrooms providing a choice of fresh or sea water. At
the tail of the train, an observation car opens onto a porch fitted
out like a balcony and crowned with a dome.

It's aboard the *San Francisco Overland Limited* that Ravel arrives in
California at the end of January. He catches his breath for a moment; his agenda is less crowded, things have calmed down quite
a bit: when he's not trying to nap under his four-poster canopy, he
spends his time in the train's club car. From San Francisco he
leaves for Los Angeles and, since mild temperatures have made
the observation car an option, he is at leisure to observe the coun-
tryside. Shaded by tall trees that look like oaks but are actually
hollies, traveling through forests of eucalypti, the train wends its
way among mountains of differing aspects, yellow rubble or
bright greenery. Approaching Los Angeles, it passes through
sparsely settled residential suburbs where each house, set here and
there, is a story (sometimes a story with swimming pool), is one
rather than tells one, and the few shops fleetingly glimpsed are the
kind of small many-colored toys that Ravel likes.

In Los Angeles he gives a concert in the ballroom of the Bilt-
more Hotel, from which he sends his brother Édouard a postcard
of this skyscraper, pierced by a pin: the front shows the hotel, and
on the back Ravel explains that the pinhole indicates his room.
It's much better than Chicago, Los Angeles: here it's summer in

midwinter, a big city brimming with flowers that we only see growing in hothouses but that here line the avenues in a hundred degrees Fahrenheit, where big palm trees are right at home. And being in the neighborhood—it isn't even an hour's drive away in not only another convertible but this time a garnet-red and lavender-blue Stutz Bearcat with whitewall tires—Ravel takes a turn around Hollywood where he meets a few stars: Douglas Fairbanks who speaks French but Charlie Chaplin not a word. All this is most entertaining to Ravel who displays a remarkably constant good humor, although his triumph is tiring and the food still just as bad.

He heads toward Seattle aboard a Southern Pacific train out of Perth, passes through Vancouver and Portland, then switches to the Union Pacific system to leave Denver—gold and silver mines, sun, pure air, altitude—for Minneapolis via Kansas City. Since the weather seems to be clouding up, however, he's afraid he'll be returning the following week to a freezing New York City.

In the end it's not that cold there for celebrating his fifty-third birthday on March 7 with quite a big crowd including Gershwin, whom he'd wanted to see again to hear him play *The Man I Love.* Which Gershwin does, of course, going all-out so that he can ask him after dinner for lessons in composition but Ravel bluntly refuses, pointing out to him that he'd risk losing his melodic spontaneity and for what, I ask you, for nothing but second-rate Ravel. Plus he doesn't like taking on pupils and after all, Gershwin—it's as if his universal success weren't enough for him anymore, he's aiming higher but lacks the tools he needs, no sense in crushing him by handing them over. In short Ravel wriggles out of it, it's getting on his nerves. And even though care was taken this evening—they're beginning to know him—to fix him a dinner he ought to enjoy, in particular red meat which he likes blue, as always here it's way overdone.

Two days later, heading south once again aboard the *Crescent Limited*, Ravel finds himself back in springtime, such a lovely summery warmth that he finds his stateroom bearable only in his shirtsleeves with all the vents open and the fan set on high. It's a trifle less hot on the balcony of the rear observation car, where Ravel dozes all day; after dinner he settles into the club car to write a few letters in which he describes in detail his complicated journey: first he'll visit New Orleans, to eat fish cooked in paper bags and drink French wine in spite of Prohibition (and if only people knew what kind of Prohibition they really had!). At around eleven o'clock, as the club car is beginning to empty out, he returns to his stateroom at the other end of the train.

Although New York had already begun to enjoy nice weather, spring flowering there lags far behind New Orleans, where Ravel spends only one day before leaving that same evening for Houston to give two concerts. At rehearsals, the instrumentalists are struck by the way he matches his suspenders to his shirt and changes colors daily: pink one time, blue the next. Everything is still going quite well, at least that's his impression, although he doesn't ask himself if the reception he's receiving accurately reflects the feeling of triumph he's been enjoying for four months now. A feeling that leads to a certain nonchalance, an increasing offhandedness in his already insecure piano playing. He thinks no one has noticed, in fact he doesn't think about it. Well, people have noticed. He doesn't know this. Even if he did he wouldn't give a goddamn.

Before the second concert, he gives a lecture at the Scottish Rite Cathedral, where he explains that he usually requires a long gestation period to compose. That during this period he begins gradually, but more and more precisely, to see the shape and over-all trajectory of the work to come. That he can be preoccupied like this for years, without setting down a single note. And that afterward the writing goes rather quickly, even though it still takes quite a bit of work to eliminate whatever is superfluous before arriving—insofar as is possible—at the intended final clarity.

That said, Ravel speeds off in a car to visit the Gulf of Mexico before bouncing back toward the Grand Canyon where, based in Phoenix, he spends one week, then heads across the continent to Buffalo aboard the *California Limited.* After which—let's cut this short—he returns to New York and then it's Montreal and on to Toronto, Milwaukee, Detroit, last hop to Boston, final swing through New York City where he embarks on the *Paris* at midnight.

He returns to Le Havre on April 27. He is in fine fettle, and above all, his little blue suitcase, emptied of its Gauloises, now contains twenty-seven thousand dollars. On the pier, the whole gang is there, keeping an eye out for him. Édouard is waiting with the Delages, Hélène as well of course, still accompanied by Marcelle Gérar and Madeleine Grey, who throw themselves at Ravel's knees to present him with a bouquet nestled in a scalloped paper-lace doily. In a jovial mood, Ravel finds it only natural that they've come to Le Havre to welcome him and it never occurs to him to thank them. Well, he simply tells them, I would really have liked to see you try not showing up.

SIX

BACK IN MONTFORT-L'AMAURY, a classic and temperate French spring provides a change from American eccentricities. Even before Ravel has opened his front door, he is greeted by flocks of birds overhead, putting the finishing touches to their recitals. From the robin to the titmouse, piping songs that Ravel has at his fingertips, lots of little fellows warble away in the trees, watched closely by his two Siamese cats.

The house itself, for all its splendid view of the valley below, is rather bizarrely slapped together. Shaped like a quarter-wheel of brie, distinctly different in aspect when seen from the street and the garden, it contains five or six rooms as cramped as nests, linked by a spindly staircase and a hallway one person wide. As Ravel himself is not tall, one may laugh at his desire for a home his own size, but he has the last laugh. First, he found something within his means, which are limited: not being rich, obliged to count costs, he would never have been able to buy the place without a small inheritance from a Swiss uncle. And besides it's the view above all that convinced him, that view over the valley discovered from the balcony: horizon almost rectilinear beneath changeable skies, long even waves of overlapping hills, foothills of grass and woods, punctiform clumps of trees, stretches of hedgerows.

True, this small dwelling is itself stuffed with small things, miniatures of all kinds, statuettes and knickknacks, music boxes and windup toys: a wooden Chinaman sticks out his tongue on demand; a sailboat rocks over cardboard waves at your pleasure; a mechanical nightingale the size of a billiard ball flaps its wings and sings whenever you like. Millefiori and bottle imps, tulip of spun glass, rose with articulated petals, boxes of colored Austrian crystal, a midget ottoman in scalloped bone-china lace. This home is equipped, moreover, with every modern comfort: vacuum cleaner and phonograph, telephone and radio.

Once the house has been inspected, the taffeta drapes in the drawing room and the green silk ones in the dining room opened, all clothing unpacked and put away, the pleasure of returning home promptly evaporates. There is a feeling of being at a loss, unsure of what to do with oneself. Too fatigued by traveling to think about resting, nerves too on edge for that, and anyway, five-thirty in the afternoon, that's no time to try sleeping, he'll never succeed—if he does it will be worse. No question either of opening a book or the piano, not focused enough for that. Nothing to tidy up in the house either, no errands to run: in preparation for her employer's return, Mme Révelot has cleaned the place from top to bottom, turned the heating back on, and re-stocked the kitchen. True, there are all those articles devoted to him over these last few months by the American newspapers, they've been cut out for him and he's kept them without much understanding what they say; he dumps them en masse into an album but that doesn't take long. There's always the possibility of strolling in the garden, a triangular, grassy, sloping space as curved as a girl's G-string. But that garden, that day—even though Ravel usually pays close attention to it, he hardly sees it at the moment, hardly takes any interest at all in the work the gardener has done while he was away. One would think he was beginning to get bored.

Now, boredom, Ravel knows it well: paired with loafing around, boredom can make him play with a diabolo-top for hours, watch his fingernails grow, make chickens out of folded paper or ducks from soft bread, inventory or even try to sort through his record collection, which runs from Albéniz to Weber, without hitting Beethoven but not excluding Vincent Scotto, Noël-Noël, or Jean Tranchant;[12] in any case he doesn't listen to his records much. Combined with the absence of projects, boredom rather often comes coupled with bouts of discouragement, pessimism, and melancholy that lead him to reproach his parents bitterly, at such moments, for not having pushed him into the grocery trade. But the boredom of this moment, utterly devoid of projects, seems unusually physical and oppressive: it's a febrile acedia, unnerving, with a feeling of loneliness that grips his throat more painfully than the knot of his polka-dotted tie. I see only one solution: to call Zogheb. It's Montfort 56, provided he's home.

On the phone, alleluia, Zogheb is home. They're happy to talk to each other, to hear each other's voice and of course we'll get together and why not right away. Five minutes later they meet on the terrace of a café near the church where, over a vermouth-cassis, Ravel talks about America to his pal who's eager to hear all about it. Jacques de Zogheb? Nobody really knows what he does. It seems he writes but no one ever knows what. He's a fellow with gleaming black hair and a matte complexion, slightly taller than Ravel but also much more robust and, like him, most particular about his clothes. What's good about him is, he knows practically nothing about music, so they can talk of other things. Yet as he's more than willing to learn about the subject, Ravel can talk music more freely, as when Zogheb asks him, Chopin, basically, who's he? It's quite simple, replies Ravel, stubbing out his cigarette: He's the greatest of the Italians. Since the vermouth-cassis, even followed by one or two more, is not enough to finish the American tale, Zogheb invites him to dinner after which fatigue from the time lag, which Ravel has never experienced before, kicks in to the point that he goes home at around eleven o'clock.

Back home, instead of wandering as usual through his house until all hours, he goes straight downstairs to his bedroom, he's that sleepy. But feeling sleepy, it's common knowledge, still doesn't mean falling asleep: too much fatigue can keep one awake. He turns the light off anyway only to switch it back on fifteen minutes later, grabs a book he opens to no effect, turns the light off then on again several times after tossing and turning in bed, the same old story. He has never slept well anyhow, most of the time going to bed late without going to sleep, then when he has barely drifted off, he always awakens too quickly. It's hardly a new problem; he's even tried to perfect a few techniques.

Technique Number 1: to make up a story and organize it, stage it in detail, as meticulously as possible, taking care to contrive conditions favorable to its growth. To create characters (not forgetting oneself in the lead role), construct sets, arrange the lights, imagine a soundtrack. Good. Now enter this scenario and develop it, control it methodically until the situation reverses itself and, taking on a life of its own, takes hold of you, inventing you in the end the way you yourself invented it. That's how, in the best of cases, this story uses what's on offer to its own advantage, becoming independent and evolving according to its own laws completely into a dream, and to dream means to sleep and off you go.

Objection: that's all very nice but to imagine that you can see sleep coming is to seriously misunderstand it. In a pinch you can feel it settling in, but you can't any more see it than you can look directly at the sun. It will be sleep that grabs you from behind, or from just out of sight. Because you don't approach sleep on the alert, peering into the distance, watching for the sudden appearance of hypnagogic visions—grids, spirals, constellations—that ordinarily herald its arrival. And if you go looking for them, these visions, if you try to induce them—they retreat, clear out, steal away, waiting until you've given up on them before mounting their attack. Or not. So.

On a Sunday three weeks later, about fifty guests show up at Montfort under threatening skies to present to Ravel, with great pomp, a bust of himself sculpted by Léon Leyritz. At first they spread out through the house, which is rather untidy, but as always, nothing is lying around in Ravel's study: it's a point of honor with him to leave no sign of work there. Neither pencil nor eraser nor ruled paper on his worktable or, beneath the portrait of his mother, on his Érard piano, always closed when he has company: nothing in my hands, nothing up my sleeves. Then, despite the gloomy weather, everyone decides to go outdoors to have a drink. Well suited to the house, the garden isn't really a large one but, semi-Japanese, it's organized around steps, paths winding among small lawns, and walks bordered with rare flowers and dwarf trees that converge on an ornamental fountain in which jiggles a thin jet of water.

So aside from Hélène, of course, and Leyritz who is a nice boy with a pleasant voice, a tiny bit affected, there are quite a few people there that you must not know, like René Kerdyck, Suzy Welty, or Pierre-Octave Ferroud, but also others of whom you have perhaps heard such as Arthur Honegger, Jacques Ibert, or the poet Léon-Paul Fargue, in short the usual friends including young Rosenthal[13] who—it's always his job—must pump on the ice-making machine for hours to keep the drinks cool. A self-proclaimed specialist in cocktails, Ravel spends an insane amount of time in the basement inventing secret recipes for weird mixtures he christens *Andalou*, *Phi-Phi*, or *Valencia*. Consumption of a certain number of them is de rigueur before posing for the photograph: it's rare to see him—always so formal—in his shirtsleeves like that, cuffs rolled up, the Gauloise always in hand, the other hand always in his pocket, surrounded by five pretty and broadly smiling women. He alone is not smiling even though everyone seems to be having a grand old time: they play blindman's buff after a luncheon with copious libations, then Ravel in fine form—borrowing Hélène's hat and Mme Gil-Marchex's coat—performs a few dance steps to general acclaim. After that it seems they'll wind up this fine Sunday in a nightclub.

Or not, according to the neighbors, the eternal neighbors. Two days later, invited to dinner by Ravel, Zogheb finds him in his kitchen with the diminutive Mme Révelot in her black dress, shoulders hunched, face impassive, attending to her ovens, back turned, seeming displeased. Since her employer also looks irritated, Zogheb asks what's going on. Tell me, Ravel blurts out, has anyone ever said unkind things about you? Zogheb replies that he has no idea, and that actually he couldn't care less. And about me, hints Ravel, you haven't heard anything? I have indeed, I'm afraid, admits Zogheb. Certain things, yes. What things? asks the other man. Well, says Zogheb, it seems that you invited fifty people to your house the day before yesterday to unveil your bust, which first off I find hardly believable considering the size of your home. True enough, admits Ravel. That's not all, says Zogheb. It would appear that afterward all these fashionable society people wound up stark naked by the end of the evening in order to, well, you see what I mean—is that what you're talking about? That's it! exclaims Ravel. That's the nasty gossip my housekeeper heard at the market. Don't you think it's a disgrace? That's not the disgrace, announces Zogheb. Well then, what is? asks Ravel in astonishment. The disgrace, replies Zogheb sternly, is always to invite me to genteel and frankly rather boring parties only to forget me the one time everyone has some fun. Ravel stiffens for a second, then turns to Mme Révelot, who hunches her shoulders a bit more. There, he barks at her, there's the reproach you've brought on me by making all that fuss. Ravel starts laughing violently, Zogheb joins in, then they fall silent.

In the days that follow, Ravel has no idea what to do. Nothing really tempts him, nothing worthwhile. He's beginning to worry seriously about this when Ida Rubinstein[14] proposes that he orchestrate a few pieces from *Iberia*, by Albéniz, to make a ballet she would dance herself. Now, Ida Rubinstein is wonderful, the kind of girl who goes lion-hunting in Africa when she's bored, the kind who calls you in the middle of the night from Amsterdam to tell you just how elegantly, this morning, seen from the airplane flying her back from Bali, the sun was rising over the Acropolis, the kind who sails off on her yacht to go halfway around the globe accompanied by her monkeys and her tame panther, not ever forgetting her cloth-of-gold pajamas, her turbans topped with aigrettes, or her bejeweled boleros. Ida Rubinstein is very tall, very thin, very beautiful, very rich, one can refuse her nothing. And well there you have it. It's a project. There's always that.

Ravel sets to work, seeming to enjoy it until the summer is in full swing: time to pay the long annual visit to the Basque country, to Saint-Jean-de-Luz near Ciboure where he was born, and spend time with his friends Gustave Samazeuilh and Marie Gaudin. Bulls, pelota and sea-bathing, Espelette peppers and the wine of Irouléguy, where Joaquin Nin[15] takes him in his Hotchkiss. They stop over in Arcachon where, when night has fallen out on the boardwalk, Nin suggests to Ravel that there might be a problem with the rights in this Albéniz project because a certain Arbos seems to have already orchestrated those pieces. What the hell do I care, says Ravel curtly, and who's this Arbos anyway? But he doesn't seem as carefree about it as all that. Noticing his increasing anxiety about this, Nin inquires into the matter with the publisher. It becomes apparent that an impregnable network of agreements, contracts, signatures, and copyrights protects *Iberia:* no one except the aforementioned Arbos has the right to work on Albéniz.

Ravel in a towering rage, frustrated and upset in Saint-Jean-de-Luz: My vacation is shot to hell, all these laws are idiotic, I need to work, I was enjoying orchestrating that, and besides—what am I going to tell Ida? She'll be furious. In any case I'm returning to Paris tomorrow, I don't want to miss July 14. Nin doesn't believe a word of it, certain that Ravel will instead make a beeline for the publisher and Ida to try to work something out. Nin is mistaken. Whenever Bastille Day rolls around, Ravel gets as giddy as a schoolgirl, can't possibly miss out on the least little street party. He scours all the neighborhoods of Paris, lingers at every terrace, where he loves to watch the couples dancing cheek-to-cheek under Chinese lanterns and listen to the orchestra, even when it's just a single accordion.

The next day, however, when Nin swings by his hotel to drive him to the station, he finds Ravel in a panic, not knowing which way to turn in the appalling disorder of his room. Shoes and suspenders, brushes and ties, toiletries and cigarette packs are in a jumble on his bed, while the train is leaving in fifteen minutes. Almost dressed, Ravel is determined to slick his hair back properly but Nin drags him firmly off to the car, along the way snatching up a few articles quickly stuffed into a suitcase. Arriving at the station just in time, he shoves Ravel onto the already moving train and, running alongside the car, sends the fortunately not too heavy suitcase flying through the window into his compartment.

Then the crisis turns out to be simply a false alarm: the elderly Arbos, apprised of the situation, graciously makes it known that he will be honored to cede to the younger man whatever rights he would like. Which speaks, after the American tour, to the glory of the younger man who promptly—a younger man's whim—drops the project. Time is pressing, however; the publisher involved needs a score for October. Fine, says Ravel: I'll just take care of it on my own. Might as well compose something myself, I'll be able to orchestrate my music faster than anyone else's. Besides, it's only a ballet, no need for form strictly speaking or development, practically no need to modulate either, just some rhythm and the orchestra. The music, this time, is of no great importance. All that's left is to get on with it.

Back in Saint-Jean-de-Luz, early in the morning, here he is about to leave for the beach with Samazeuilh. Wearing a golden-yellow bathrobe over a black bathing costume with shoulder straps and coiffed in a scarlet bathing cap, Ravel lingers a moment at the piano, playing a phrase over and over on the keyboard with one finger. Don't you think this theme has something insistent about it? he asks Samazeuilh. Then off he goes to swim. After which, sitting on the sand in the July sunshine, he mentions that same phrase again. It would be good to make something out of it. He might, for example, try to repeat it a few times but without developing the phrase, just swelling the orchestra and graduating it as best and for as long as he can. Right? Who knows, he says, standing up to go for another swim, it might work as well as *La Madelon*.[16] But it will work out a lot better, Maurice: it will work out a hundred thousand times better than *La Madelon*.

The holidays are over. He's sitting at his piano, home alone, a score in front of him, cigarette between his lips, hair as impeccably combed as ever. Under his dressing gown with its bright lapels and matching pocket handkerchief, he is wearing a gray-striped shirt and a bronze-colored tie. Positioned for a chord, his left hand rests on the keyboard while his right, armed with a metal mechanical pencil wedged between thumb and index, notes on the score what the left has just produced. As usual he is behind in his work and the telephone has just rung: the publisher reminding him once again to hurry. He must provide as soon as possible the rehearsal dates for this work-in-progress, which he has announced but about which nothing is known. Ravel smiles but it doesn't show. All right, they want to rehearse, they're really anxious to rehearse, well then fine, they'll rehearse. Rehearse: Middle French *rehercier,* to repeat. They'll get their fill and more, *de la répétition.*

Then, as always when he is alone, he dines at the drop-leaf table, facing the wall. As he greedily eats his meat, his false teeth sound like castanets or a machine gun, the noise echoing in the confined space. As he eats he thinks about what he's working on. He has always liked automatons and machines, visiting factories, industrial landscapes; he remembers those of Belgium and the Rhineland when he traveled through them on a river yacht more than twenty years ago: the cities bristling with chimneys, the furnace domes belching flames with blue and reddish-brown smoke, the foundry castles, the incandescent cathedrals, the symphonies of conveyor belts, whistles, and hammer-blows beneath the red sky.

Perhaps he comes by it honestly, this taste for machinery, his father having sacrificed the trumpet and flute to an engineer's career that led him to invent among other things a steam generator fueled by mineral oils and applied to locomotion, plus a machine gun, a supercharged two-stroke engine, a machine to manufacture paper bags, and a vehicle with which he devised an acrobatic act called the Whirlwind of Death. Anyway, there's a factory that Ravel currently likes to look at, on the Vésinet road, right after the bridge at Rueil. It gives him ideas. So there it is: he is busy composing something based on the assembly line.

Assembly and repetition: the composition is completed in October after a month of work hampered only by a splendid cold picked up on a trip through Spain, beneath the coconut palms of Malaga. He knows perfectly well what he has made: there's no form, strictly speaking, no development or modulation, just some rhythm and arrangement. In short it's a thing that self-destructs, a score without music, an orchestral factory without a purpose, a suicide whose weapon is the simple swelling of sound. Phrase run into the ground, thing without hope or promise: there, he says, is at least one piece Sunday orchestras won't have the cheek to put on their programs. But none of that's important: the thing was only made to be danced. The choreography, the lighting, the scenery will be what carry off the tedious repetitions of that phrase. After he has finished, when he passes the factory on the Vésinet road one day with his brother, Ravel says to him, you see, there it is, the *Boléro* plant.

Well, things don't go at all as planned. The first time it's danced, it's somewhat disconcerting but it works. Later on in the concert hall, however, is when it works terrifically. It works extraordinarily. This object without hope enjoys a triumph that stuns everyone, beginning with its creator. True, when an old lady in the audience complains loudly at the end of one of the first performances that he's a madman, Ravel nods: There's one of them at least who understands, he says, just to his brother. Eventually, this success will trouble him. That such a pessimistic project would meet with popular acclaim that is soon so universal and long-lasting that the piece becomes one of the world's warhorses—well it's enough to make one wonder but—above all—to go straight to the point. To those bold enough to ask him what he considers his masterpiece, he shoots back: It's *Boléro*, what else; unfortunately, there's no music in it.

Although he feels somewhat disdainful of the piece, that doesn't mean anyone should take it lightly. The world must understand as well that one shouldn't trifle with its tempo. When Toscanini conducts it after his own fashion, two times too fast and *accelerando*, Ravel goes to see him after the concert. That wasn't my tempo, he points out to him coldly. Toscanini leans toward him, raising the eyebrows on that long façade he uses for a face, making it even longer. When I play that in your tempo, he says, it falls flat. Fine, replies Ravel, then don't play it. But you don't know a thing about your own music, bristles Toscanini's mustache; it was the only way to put the piece over. When Ravel gets home, without speaking to anyone, he writes to Toscanini. No one knows what he told him in that letter.

Well, he has just finished that little business in C major, which he doesn't realize will be his crowning glory, when he's invited to Oxford. So here he is emerging from the Sheldonian Theater into the courtyard of the Bodleian Library in frock coat and striped trousers, wing collar and tie, his patent-leather shoes without which he is nothing, draped in a toga with a cap on his head, laughing and standing as straight as possible. Hands closed into fists, his arms hanging alongside his short body, in the photo he looks a tiny bit silly. Eight years earlier, he'd made a huge to-do over refusing the Légion d'honneur but an honorary doctorate from Oxford University with a eulogy in Latin to top it off, that's not something one turns down, plus it's worth it just to set out again on a little trip through Spain to recuperate.

One evening in his hotel, rather enjoying being in Saragossa, he is alone in his room, leaning back in his armchair in front of the open window. He has taken off his shoes and placed his bare feet on the guardrail. He contemplates those feet, at the end of which his ten toes move all on their own, wiggling among themselves as if signaling to him, sending him messages of solidarity. We are your toes, we are all here, we're counting on you and you know you can also count on us the way you do on your fingers.

He thinks he can count on them but two days later, attempting to play his *Sonatine* at the embassy in Madrid, he goes directly from the exposition to the coda of the finale, skipping the minuet movement. One may think what one likes of this incident. One may believe in a lapse of memory. One may suppose that it wearies him, having to play something more than twenty years old over and over forever. One may also imagine that, before a less-than-attentive audience, he prefers to rush through the performance. But one may also speculate that, for the first time in public, something really is going wrong.

SEVEN

TECHNIQUE NUMBER 2: While spending hours tossing and turning in bed, seek the best position, the ideal accommodation of the organism called Ravel to the piece of furniture called Ravel's bed, the most even breathing, the perfect placement of the head upon the pillow, that state in which the body becomes confused with then fused with its couch, a fusion capable of opening one of the doors to sleep. From then on Ravel need only wait for the latter to come get him, watching for this arrival as if for an invited guest.

Objection: on the one hand, as previously noted, it is this very waiting, this position as lookout and the alertness it entails— even if he tries to ignore them—that risk preventing him from sleeping. Moreover, once this position is found, the encouraging torpor that follows, holding out the dazzling prospect of sleep, frequently breaks down: a little short circuit or loose wire can turn up who knows where, and everything must be redone. Even worse, this fresh start now requires recovering a little lost ground, it's discouraging; Ravel lights his bedside lamp, then a cigarette, which he stubs out after a few coughs only to light another one and it's endless.

He could perhaps try sleeping with someone, after all. At times sleep is easier when one is less lonely in a bed. He could always take a shot at that. But no, nothing doing. No one knows whether he ever loved, amorously, anyone—man or woman—at all. We do know that when he summoned the courage one day to propose marriage to a friend, she burst out laughing, exclaiming in front of everyone that he was crazy. We know that when he tried with Hélène, asking her in a roundabout way if she wouldn't like to live in the country, she also declined the offer, although more gently. But when a third woman, as tall and imposing as he is short and slender, made him the same offer in the other direction, we also know that he was the one who laughed till he cried.

We know that young Rosenthal found him, one time, in a *brasserie* at the Porte Champerret, where Ravel seemed to be on excellent or at least quite familiar terms with a group of whores who'd set up headquarters there. We know that this same Rosenthal was able to overhear a telephone call between Ravel and one of the girls, who was very upset that he preferred giving Rosenthal his lesson to sharing a little of his bed with her. We know that one day, taking leave of Leyritz, Ravel mentioned casually that he was off to the brothel, but perhaps he was joking about it. So we know few things, although we can assume some of them, including this taste—perhaps for lack of anything better—for brief encounters. In short we know nothing, practically nothing except that one day, when Marguerite Long[17] encourages him to marry, he addresses the subject of love for once—and once and for all: this feeling, in his opinion, never rises above licentiousness.

Let's drop the subject. Everything went so well last year at Oxford with his honorary doctorate that he is invited back to England. Ravel arrives there at almost the same time as Wittgenstein, who comes in from Austria to receive a doctorate as well but in his case from Cambridge and in philosophy. While it's highly unlikely that Ravel ever met Ludwig Wittgenstein, at least he crosses his path, since three weeks later, it's in Vienna that he becomes acquainted with his older brother. The pianist Paul Wittgenstein, made prisoner in Russia, deported to Siberia, returned from the front minus his right arm. Undiscouraged by that loss, he has logically devoted himself to what has been written so far for the left hand alone. Since this repertoire is limited, however—Reger, Saint-Saëns, Schubert transcribed by Liszt, and Bach by Brahms—he has decided to commission pieces for that hand from a few composers of his day. As it happens, Ravel runs into him at a concert, at which Paul Wittgenstein plays something by Richard Strauss conceived especially for the left hand. Paul Wittgenstein: rather a good pianist; the beefy, pretty face of an old young man, albeit a bit impassive; not bad but nowhere near as handsome as his brother. They say hello, delighted to meet you, and leave it at that.

Back in France, things aren't going very well. Ravel is still smoking too much, still as bored as ever, still sleeping as poorly as usual, once again always dead tired, constantly tormented by chronic swollen glands and other minor problems. Above all, after the strange business of *Boléro*, he doesn't much know what to do with himself anymore. True, he does have some vague projects brewing, an old idea about a concerto but it's rather traditional, a few idle thoughts about *Jeanne d'Arc*[18] but they're tiresome, some attempts at orchestration but they go nowhere, a stab at dusting off *Le Roi malgré lui* but—enough said. Better to go off on holiday again, spend the whole summer in the Basque country and think about other things.

And at the end of the summer, while he is on his balcony reading the not so glad tidings in *Le Populaire*, a note from Wittgenstein arrives commissioning a concerto for his remaining hand. That's when no one knows what gets into Ravel: he doesn't just accept the commission—instead of writing one concerto, he undertakes in secret to compose two at the same time, one for the left hand in D major and another in G that will finally realize one of his longtime projects. While one will be for Wittgenstein, the other will be for him, no one but him, and besides, he thinks, he'll play it himself. Until that day, one after the other, he has produced only single specimens; this is the first time that he intends to give birth, simultaneously, to twins.

But they will be heterozygotic twins, sharing only a birthday, nothing in the way of resemblance. He begins by sketching out his *Piano Concerto in G major*, then sets it aside to complete his commission. Once the question of the left hand has been rather swiftly settled, in a logical nine months, he turns back to the other work but this time things do not run smoothly. He's hung up, has heaps of trouble, just can't figure out how to finish it. It's complicated, after all, a delicate proposition, given that the concerto wasn't conceived for the piano but against it. Fine, he tells Zogheb: Since I can't manage to finish this thing for two hands, I've decided not to sleep, I mean not even for one second, you understand. I won't rest until this work is finished—be it in this world or the next.

When it's completed at last, Marguerite Long, informed immediately, begins to sight-read it and not without difficulty: when the composer isn't breathing down her neck, constantly correcting her, he's pestering her over the phone. Hesitantly, she tells him of her misgivings about his second movement, about how hard it is for the performer to hold up under that slow progression, she says, that long, flowing phrase. Flowing? Ravel starts shouting. What do you mean, flowing? But I wrote it two measures at a time and it almost killed me! Point taken, but he did the whole thing rather fast, all in all, taking only a little more than a year to polish off his double idea.

When he decided that his *Piano Concerto for the Left Hand* was done, Ravel invited its commissioner to Montfort to present it to him. Paul Wittgenstein still seems just as impassive: small glasses and German brush cut; a stiff, brusque bearing; the end of his empty right jacket sleeve tucked into his pocket. Fortunately he's not staying for lunch; Ravel is already imagining how to go about cutting his meat for him and foreseeing that a brief glance from his guest will warn him off. They stick to discussing the results of the commission. After laying out the composition of the orchestra and the basic atmosphere of each movement, Ravel plays the solo part with both hands, and not very well. First off, Wittgenstein finds him a rather poor pianist, and as for the work itself, proud of the fact that he was never taught to pretend, he doesn't hide his opinion that it's not too hot. Ravel tries to conceal his disappointment by fiddling with a Gauloise, rolling it between his fingers quite a while before placing it between his lips, smoking it silently for as long as that takes. Wittgenstein then coldly slips the score into his left pocket before taking his leave.

But this wound is only a minor splinter. He can see for himself these days that his fame is solidifying, that he's played everywhere, that the newspapers speak only of him. No one has ever seen anything like it, so that a *Paris-Soir* columnist even exclaims that the composer of the *Valses nobles et sentimentales* can legitimately boast of having justified the invention of those extra flap-seats in theaters. He has become so unassailable that young composers are growing restless, raising a ruckus, even vilifying him in the press, but it seems that once more he doesn't give a goddamn. One evening when he and young Rosenthal are attending a performance of a ballet by Darius Milhaud, he applauds until it hurts, finding it absolutely wonderful, bravo, magnificent, superb.

Wait a minute, his neighbor tells him, don't you know what Milhaud says about you? He spends his time dragging you through the mud. He's not wrong, Ravel points out: When you're young, that is what you must do. Another evening, with Hélène, another ballet, this time it's by Georges Auric and he finds it just as wonderful, so well done that he wants to go compliment the composer. What, says Hélène, you'd go congratulate Auric after what he's written about you? Why not, he replies. He lashes out at Ravel? Well, he's right to lash out at Ravel. If he didn't lash out at Ravel, he'd be cranking out Ravel and that's enough, now, of Ravel.

And speaking of celebrations, in mid-August a festival in his honor is organized in Saint-Jean-de-Luz, during which his name will be given to the quay where he was born. His piano, his bathing suit, and his daily routines are all waiting for him; the ceremony goes well, too, even though the novelist Claude Farrère (white beard and deep voice, classic merchant-marine-officer profile) somewhat botches his speech—before which, in any case, Ravel makes himself scarce. Let's go have a cherry brandy instead, he tells Robert Casadesus,[19] taking him by the arm; I don't want to be fool enough to attend the laying of my own plaque. On the other hand, he takes a keen interest in the pelota tournament that winds up the festivities, and after which, in his suit, bareheaded, the eternal Gauloise in hand, he poses for the photographer among four colossal and thuggish-looking *pelotari* wearing white and topped with berets. This time, in the photo, amid the stony-faced colossi, he is the only one smiling. Even though the final event of the day will be a concert of his works, given to benefit various charitable enterprises, as usual he's late; still not there, he makes everyone wait a long time for him, arriving at last only to discover in horror that he has forgotten his fancy pocket handkerchief and that's a whole new song and dance. Casadesus offers to lend him his own hankie but it's no use, Ravel says that's impossible. Well, of course that's impossible, since it doesn't have the same initials on it. But after all it's not the end of the world since he takes off the next day in the Hispano of Edmond Gaudin, Marie's father, to watch the bullfighting in the arena at San Sebastián by Marcial Lalanda (one ear and *division*), Enrique Torres (ovation and whistles), and Nicanor Villalta[20] (silence and silence).

Back in Paris, his fame makes him feel like working harder than ever. Tired of shuttling between Montfort and Paris, he sets up a small studio where he can work in his brother's house in Levallois. It's Leyritz who designs the décor in a style that's half ocean liner, half dentist's office: nickel-steel furniture and tubular chairs, circle rugs, mobile bar with high stools, shaker, tall glasses, and bottles in every possible color. No paintings on the walls, not even fakes as in Montfort, just a few Japanese prints and some photographs by Man Ray. Anyway, Ravel will hardly ever set foot there.

Perhaps his shining glory produces a slight giddiness as well, because now this man who is usually ironic and rather aloof is beginning to lose his grip. While hard at work these past few months, even before he had finished composing his two concertos, he had come up with a plan to go on a world tour with the one written for two hands: his own hands. He wants to present it on every continent, the five parts of the world, all five, he insists to anyone who will listen. But meanwhile, his body has grown still weaker, he's not up to it, the doctors intervene. Worried about his health, they firmly oppose this plan. Gently does it. Threats and prognoses, warnings, prescriptions and treatments. Injections of serum and complete rest.

Not for long: it will be against medical advice that he stubbornly sets off on tour, he and his concerto, with Marguerite Long bringing up the rear. In the end she is the one who will play it, not himself as he'd hoped, despite his killing efforts trying to achieve the required virtuosity, hours spent breaking his fingers on the *Études* of Liszt and Chopin to improve his skill. But in vain: he is truly forced to admit that this time, his music is beyond his reach, much too complicated for his hands, which will make do with directing it. He must therefore set out with Marguerite, which isn't so bad with regard to the keyboard but a lot less jolly with regard to life because she's impossible, bossy, full of herself, the kind of governess you get saddled with on every vacation, not to mention that she's a real eyesore. Plus it won't be the five parts of the world, they're just doing Europe although they are doing a good twenty cities. As always, however, it will go very well: from London to Budapest and from Prague to The Hague, with him at the podium and Marguerite at the piano they knock them dead wherever they go.

On the train to Vienna, he pulls the same stunt as in Chicago, realizing that he has forgotten his patent-leather shoes again: no question of appearing without them. It's not that serious, you'll find the same ones there, says Marguerite, unaware that such a small size can't be ferreted out just anywhere. This time it isn't a devoted singer but, once Paris is alerted, the engineer of the following train who manages to retrieve them. In Vienna, Ravel is invited with Marguerite to a big dinner party followed by a musical soirée in their honor in the home of Paul Wittgenstein, during which the latter, the commissioner and dedicatee of the work, will play the concerto with his own hand. The dinner proceeds like others of its kind, meaning that initially it's a dreaded chore but one gets dressed, arrives, is introduced to scads of people with names no sooner barely heard than forgotten, bored stiff at first one then gets used to it, the alcohol loosens things up, this could even be fun and lo and behold, after an hour or two everything's wonderful and wild horses couldn't drag one away.

In short it's always the same except that this evening, sitting to the right of Wittgenstein, Marguerite hears him disclose to her that he had to make certain changes in the concerto she doesn't yet know about. Supposing that the pianist's infirmity has led him to simplify a few things, she suggests nevertheless that he warn Ravel about these adjustments, but Wittgenstein doesn't listen to her. They rise from the table, they proceed to the concert.

As soon as the performance begins, with Marguerite following the score of the concerto, this time sitting next to its creator, she sees in his ever more aghast expression the distressing consequences of the one-armed pianist's initiatives. The thing is, Wittgenstein has not simplified the work at all to adapt it to his abilities, on the contrary: he must have seen an opportunity to show, handicapped though he might be, how very good he is. Instead of addressing the work and serving it as best he can, there he is piling stuff on, adding arpeggios here, extra measures there, embroidering trills, rhythmic shimmies, and other performance embellishments that no one had asked him for, appoggiaturas and gruppetti, racing up the keyboard into the high notes at every opportunity to show how skilful he is, how clever he is, how supple he still is, and how he's telling you all to go to hell. Ravel's face is white.

At the end of the concert, anticipating trouble, Marguerite immediately attempts to create a diversion by talking about something else with the ambassador, but in vain: Ravel slowly approaches Wittgenstein with a look no one has seen on his face since he advanced upon Toscanini. That won't do, he says icily. That won't do at all. That's not it at all. Wittgenstein tries to defend himself: Listen, I'm an old pianist and frankly, it doesn't sound good. Well, I'm an old orchestrator, replies Ravel, growing more and more frosty, and I can tell you that it sounds fine. As for the silence that settles over the room at those words, it sounds even louder. Malaise beneath the moldings; embarrassment below the stucco. The shirt fronts of tuxedos blanch; the fringes on evening gowns freeze; the butlers study their shoes. Without a word Ravel puts on his coat and leaves early, dragging after him a bewildered Marguerite. Vienna, a January evening, filthy weather but so what: he sends away the car placed at his disposal by the embassy and, counting on a short walk in the snow to calm down, returns to the hotel on foot.

But he is still just as upset the next day while waiting for the train home, Gauloise in his right hand while the left, gloved, keeps absentmindedly crumpling his right glove. At the moment of departure, on the station platform, Marguerite rummages through her purse with increasing panic and grows pale. It's silly, she stammers, scrabbling with her fingers at the bottom of the purse—I can't find them. What, snaps Ravel, what can't you find? The tickets, says Marguerite. They must be around somewhere, they've got to be here, I mean wherever could I have put them? You really are an idiot, Marguerite, says Ravel, coldly exasperated. A fucking idiot, he adds deliberately, folding a newspaper over twice. Marguerite blinks rather a lot, startled by this sudden vulgarity, which isn't like him but continues: That bitch, she's lost the tickets, he groans to himself—she always has to forget something. Here they are! exclaims Marguerite at last, showing him the tickets tucked into her fur muff: I put them there so they'd be safer. Immediately recovering his relative composure and detachment, Ravel returns to his newspaper, showing no further interest in his escort, who makes a few chatty remarks while flicking the tag ends of worried looks his way. He doesn't even glance up at the arrival on the run of a breathless Artur Rubinstein, informed at the last minute of Ravel's presence in Vienna and certainly hoping to shake the master's hand before his departure, but the master jumps onto the train as if he didn't exist.

Still, it is better that Marguerite should take care of the tickets because he is forgetting everything: his appointments, his patent-leather shoes, his luggage, his watch, his keys, his passport, his mail. Which can pose problems: welcome everywhere, sought after by the powers-that-be, entertained on all sides, Ravel tends to let official invitations languish in the neglect of his jacket pockets, and he is expected in vain. The king of Romania doesn't take it too badly, but the Polish prime minister raises one hell of a fuss. Diplomatic incidents, panic in the consulates of France, ambassadorial interventions. Ravel has always forgotten every-thing, always been absentminded, subject to memory lapses re-garding proper names in particular, often relying on images to designate places or people as familiar to him as Mme Révelot: the lady who takes care of my house, you know, with the nasty dispo-sition. And even Marguerite herself: the woman who doesn't play the piano too well, you see who I mean, her husband died in the war. Although Marguerite knows all that, she still thinks he's for-getting more and more things. For her part, Hélène noticed a year ago that Ravel is now revealing, from time to time, a kind of ab-sence before his own music.

Nevertheless he doesn't forget what counts the most in his

eyes: as soon as he returns to France, he bluntly opposes the coming of Wittgenstein, who'd confidently seen himself paying a little visit to Paris. The composer sends him a short note pointing out that his interpretation is based on counterfeiting, and enjoining him firmly to pledge that henceforward he will play the work strictly as it was written. When Wittgenstein, offended, writes back that performers must not be slaves, Ravel's reply is three words long: Performers are slaves.

So. He is fifty-seven years old. Thirteen years earlier he wrapped up his works for piano with *Frontispice*, which consists of no more than fifteen measures, lasts no longer than two minutes, but requires no less than five hands. He settled the formal hash of the sonata and the quartet. After pushing his powers of orchestration to the limit—at the risk of smashing his toy—with *Boléro*, he has just solved the concerto problem, the only one he had always put off confronting. Now what? Well, these days, two projects. One is some music for a film about Don Quixote that Pabst was supposed to film with Feodor Chaliapin in the title role and Paul Morand doing the dialogue. About the other one, which for the moment bears the code name *Dédale 39*, we know only what Ravel is willing to say about it one day to Manuel De Falla: it was supposed to be an airplane in the key of C.

EIGHT

PARIS, AN OCTOBER NIGHT, one in the morning. In front of the Théâtre des Champs-Elysées, Jean Delfini, florid complexion and pale cap, has just taken a fare on board his taxi, a Delahaye 109. The passenger gives him an address, Hôtel d'Athènes, 21 Rue d'Athènes, and the cab sets out, it's not a long trip. In the back seat, the passenger watches the streets slip by, glances at the driver behind his glass partition, and then, increasingly absorbed by an idea, stops considering the scenery. They have almost arrived; they're going down the Rue d'Amsterdam, they're about to turn left into the Rue d'Athènes when another taxi speeds out of the intersection, this one a Renault Celtaquatre driven by Henri Lacep, sallow complexion and checkered cap.

The lateral collision is quite violent: the impact breaks the glass partition inside the taxi into a two-edged blade that attempts to cut the passenger Ravel in half. Meeting with only partial success, it merely staves in three ribs—so that he feels a brutal dent in his chest, like an inside-out bump—and shatters three teeth while shards of glass tear busily at his face, especially the nose, one eyebrow, and the chin. The authorities open up the closest pharmacy to give the passenger first-aid before taking him to the Hôpital Beaujon, where he is stitched up and allowed to return to his hotel. The next day, however, since he seems to be suffering from internal injuries, his doctor prefers to send him to a clinic on the Rue Blomet, where he can be kept under observation.

During the next three months, Ravel does absolutely nothing. He has been examined, treated, bandaged, and fitted out with new dentures. Cared for attentively, he remains stupefied. He does not say much and never complains except to remark, from time to time, that his thoughts occasionally fail him, that they don't always develop as usual. Although he has often appeared distracted, such episodes are in fact becoming more frequent. Every morning, someone brings him *Le Populaire,* which he used to read religiously from first page to last, but now he seems less interested in the paper, simply skimming it abstractedly. Since he has been working hard these last few years, his doctors have been constant in their admonitions: given his chronic fatigue, his condition was not going to improve. Now, after the accident, he seems to have greatly deteriorated. While they put him through various tests, he finally explains that it's as if his ideas, whatever they are, always remained trapped in his brain. That's completely normal after such a shock, and one should expect that this confusion will pass. The doctors examine him some more; they examine him in vain. Everyone close to him recommends a different treatment, each one a sovereign remedy. Electricity, injections, hypnosis, homeopathy, physical therapy, positive thinking, enough drugs to stun an ox, but nothing, apparently, works.

Three months having past, with stubborn Wittgenstein back in Paris after all, Ravel's condition seems somewhat improved. He even appears to have made peace with the crippled veteran—or else he couldn't care less about all that at this point—since he agrees to conduct, Salle Pleyel, the Orchestre Symphonique de Paris while the other man performs the concerto to which he has exclusive rights for six years. Which isn't enough to make Wittgenstein, bending deeply over his instrument, his empty sleeve as always tucked into his pocket, abstain from embellishing the score to his taste. He still takes liberties, indulges in virtuosic showboating, stepping up the fioritura and ripple-effects, ornamenting phrases that had never hurt a soul, his left hand obstinately straying toward the right side of the keyboard where it just doesn't belong. Apparently indifferent to this, Ravel stands at the podium, beating time and, as always when he conducts, getting a bit balled up in his movements. He gives the impression of not being completely present. What's more, since the baton passes from his right hand to his left when he turns the pages of the score, one may infer that he no longer conducts his work by heart.

Still overtired, he takes another vacation in Saint-Jean-de-Luz. Things always settle down when he goes back where he was born:

the ocean stretches out languorously, a pure sun sits in the vast sky, Samazeuilh and Marie Gaudin are there to welcome him, and yet it's during that summer that everything begins to fall seriously apart. Now certain gestures ordinarily accomplished swiftly and automatically begin to slow down or go astray. Writing, for example: Ravel, a man so concerned with form and style, seems to be having trouble getting words down even when making a list of errands. One Sunday at the bullfights with the Gaudins, without being able to explain just what he's looking for, he hunts through his pockets for a long time, then when Edmond pulls a cigarette from his, Ravel pounces on it: that's what it was. There is also the beach where, rather a good swimmer, he has always loved to venture far out into the waves, but now he says he can no longer execute certain movements in the water: they become different, go in unexpected directions. And still at the shore, when he tries to teach Marie the art of skipping stones, the action goes awry, sending the missile into his friend's face.

Three days after that incident, stubbornly refusing to stop swimming, he heads out into the open water and doesn't come back. A rescue party finds him floating on his back, letting himself drift while awaiting help. Brought back to safety and asked how he feels, he replies simply that he has forgotten how to swim. As for the doctors, not knowing what to think, they suggest that he continue his vacation in cooler weather, exchanging the Atlantic for the English Channel, for example: the beaches up north, they say, are much more invigorating. Arrangements are made to have him invited to Le Touquet, and in fact after a month he seems to be doing better. He can go home.

Perhaps he is doing a little better but he can also see that his handwriting is going downhill, losing its elegance to become hesitant, clumsy, heading toward illegibility. Since the surrealists have recently been doing their damnedest to stir things up, they decide to invite some celebrities to the office of *Minotaure*[21] to take part in one of the group's solemn pranks: this time taking the prints of famous hands and having them analyzed by an expert. Some rather diverse personalities are there, from Duchamp to Huxley and Gide to Saint-Exupéry. Even though Breton is highly suspicious of music—unless of course he just doesn't understand it at all—he has insisted that Ravel participate in this event, the only musician invited. Ravel, who seems back in form, is quite pleased to take part in this extravaganza. He arrives smiling, hair as impeccable as ever, double-breasted charcoal gray suit, bright-eyed and sprightly, rather moved to find himself with the surrealists, who may interest him more than he lets on, and he willingly plays his part: the expert places Ravel's hands on a plate coated with lampblack, then on some white paper, and that's that.

There's a little more to come, however: they must all then sign their own handprints. Well, when Ravel's turn comes and someone hands him an old-fashioned nib pen, he shrinks back. I can't, he says simply, I can't sign. My brother will send you my signature tomorrow. Then, turning to Valentine Hugo[22] who has come with him: Let's go, Valentine, let's leave quickly. Emerging silently into a pouring rain, Ravel climbs hastily into a taxi that drives off. Valentine is left standing on the sidewalk. The surrealists look at one another. As for the expert, it's a woman, Dr. Lotte Wolff. Her commentary has been preserved: He's a complete idiot.

Shortly afterward, taking advantage of the presence in Paris of the Galimir Quartet, the producer Canetti has proposed to Polydor that they record Ravel's *String Quartet.* He lets the composer know that he would appreciate having him come supervise the recording sessions. Fine, says Ravel, all right. Once settled in the control room, he watches the procedure without trying to direct it. He approves or not of what he hears but from a distance, occasionally saying that it's good, sometimes less so, sometimes that they must do it again. He specifies a few details, amending a slight liberty taken with a measure, correcting a tempo. After each movement, when they have played back the wax masters, they offer to do it over if he wishes, but since he doesn't wish to that much, the whole affair is wrapped up that afternoon. When they have finished, while the musicians are putting their instruments into their cases before putting themselves into their coats, Ravel turns to Canetti: That was nice, he says, really nice, remind me again who the composer is. One is not obliged to believe this story.

Since new examinations reveal no apparent organic lesion, he is sent to the Swiss mountains to rest. He has already experienced mountains in that guise, having spent a month after the war in a sanatorium to be treated for tuberculosis, never labeled as such and for which sun baths were the preferred remedy in those days. This time the prescription is to soak in nice hot water scented with pine bath oil every evening. Since he has to write his friends the Delages, who are expecting to hear from him, they finally become worried when no letter arrives. When they receive it at last, they go to Switzerland to see Ravel, who must then explain what happened: it had taken him eight days to write that letter, forced as he was to look up all the words in the Larousse dictionary so that he could write them down.

That's where we are. The stay in Switzerland has not helped at all. When he goes to a concert where one of his works is played, he still sometimes asks if it really is by him or, which isn't any better, he murmurs to himself that, still and all, it was lovely. Since he now knows that he can't write his name at all anymore, when young people rush up to him brandishing their pens like weapons, looking for an autograph when he leaves after a concert, escorted by Hélène, he passes through their midst like a robot, seeming to neither see nor hear them and suffering even more from this apparent disdain, put on for his protection, than from his awareness of his illness. Soon, no longer able to love anything but solitude, he spends hours in an armchair on his balcony at Montfort, gazing out at the valley he had moved there to admire. Hélène joins him outdoors, worries about him, asks what he's doing there. He replies simply that he's waiting, but without saying for what. He lives in a fog that each day stifles him a little more even though one activity persists: he goes for a long walk in the woods every day. He never gets lost there. But it's the world he's losing, and its objects: dining one evening with his publisher, what does he do but pick up the fork by its tines, realize this right away, and dart a quick look of distress at Marguerite, who is close by.

In short, things aren't going well at all. Ida Rubinstein becomes concerned and involved. Ida is no less tall, thin, beautiful, and rich than she is generous, enough to think that Ravel must have a change of scenery and to start taking care of this. It's a grand trip to Spain and then Morocco that she organizes for him, and it's Leyritz who will be his companion. Let's set out. In Tangier, things seem to be looking up already. In Marrakesh, for three weeks he roams the souks in all directions without any more getting lost than he does in the forest of Rambouillet, and back at the hotel, he manages to write three measures in the presence of Leyritz, who regains hope. Ravel is always welcomed and entertained wherever he goes, to the point of even involuntary homage, as on the day when, in an ocean of bicyclists, he seems to have heard a telegraph messenger open a path for himself by whistling *Boléro*—there again, no one is obliged to believe this story. In Fez, he is received by the French diplomatic representative who, while showing him around the city, suggests that it might prove inspiring to him. Oh, says Ravel, if I were to write something Arab, it would be much more Arab than all this. Leyritz reports back on everything by postcard to Ida Rubinstein who, for her part, telephones every day. Leyritz declares that all is well: Ravel seems quite pleased with his reception, is working a little, has even written to his brother. Leyritz tries to be reassuring but in truth Ravel is always prostrate with fatigue, irritated at everything, barely speaks at all and feels more than ever shut out of the world, especially of a world so swirling with dust, light, and movement. It is true that upon his return via Spain, once again he seems better. Attending the funeral of Dukas, Ravel even turns to Koechlin:[23] I wrote down a theme, he assures him; I can still write music. But this time he is the one nobody is obliged to believe.

Not obliged because it's happening fast and just gets worse: he now has trouble controlling most of his movements, has lost his sense of touch, can barely read or write at all anymore, and expresses himself with ever greater difficulty, constantly confusing words, with fewer and fewer of them at his command. As for music, although he can still sing or play a little from memory, and recognize works people arrange for him to hear, he can no longer read a score or decipher it at the piano. Not to mention sleep, which is still in short supply.

Technique Number 3: To try listing things. To remember for example all the beds in which he has slept since childhood. The task is important, it can take some time; whenever he does this he finds new beds in his memory—it takes so much time that it becomes boring: he can count on this boredom as a soporific factor.

Objection: this boredom can also keep Ravel awake, lead him to ask himself unexpected questions, so that he remains alert. He might also handle things poorly: sometimes a torpor sets in to which he should surrender, but instead he resists it. So strong is his desire to sleep that he observes the approach of slumber too nervously, even if he can feel its imminent arrival: this clinical attention staves off drowsiness when it's almost there, and he has to start all over again. It's just that one can't do everything at once, right?—always the same old story: it's impossible to fall asleep while keeping a sharp eye on sleep.

NINE

In any case, he has always been delicate. From peritonitis to tuberculosis and from Spanish flu to chronic bronchitis, and even though he holds himself as straight as an "i" buttoned up tight in his perfectly tailored clothes, his weary body has never been robust. Nor has his mind, either, steeped in sadness and boredom, although he never lets this show, and is never allowed to forget himself in sleep, which is strictly off-limits. This, however, is different: now he can never find the comb sitting in front of him on the dressing table, can no longer knot his tie without help, can't manage to fix his cufflinks all by himself.

People try to amuse him, they take him to concerts as much as possible, but he melts into the background in his seat, calm and motionless as if he were not there, already dead. When Toscanini returns to Paris, they manage to convince Ravel to go listen to him conduct one of his works. Somewhat guardedly, he goes, appears moved by the applause for the orchestra and conductor but, dug in at the back of his box, refuses to go congratulate him. When his companions are surprised, disappointed that he will not, by showing his pleasure, erase the old disagreement over *Boléro,* Ravel says no: he never answered my letter. As he is leaving the theater, a couple comes over to him. Their faces remind him vaguely of something, but what . . . *Cher maître,* they say to him, do you remember when you used to play *Daphnis* on our piano, a few years ago? Yes, yes, yes, says Ravel tonelessly, in a voice completely cut off from his thoughts, without seeming to have any idea who the couple are.

Although he no longer recognizes many people, he notices everything. He can see that his movements miss their targets, that he grasps a knife by its blade, that he raises the lighted end of his cigarette to his lips only to correct himself immediately every time: No, he then murmurs to himself, not like that. He's well aware that one doesn't cut one's nails that way, or put on glasses like that, and although he gets them on anyway to try to read *Le Populaire,* the muscles of his eyes won't even let him follow the print anymore. He observes all that clearly, the subject of his collapse as well as its attentive spectator, buried alive in a body that no longer responds to his intelligence, watching a stranger live inside him.

It's tragic, really, what's happening to me, he tells Marguerite. Be patient, she always replies, it won't last. Just wait a bit. And besides, look at Verdi, he had to wait until he was eighty to compose *Falstaff.* But when Ravel continues to grieve she points out to him that even if he can't compose anything else, his oeuvre is there. His oeuvre has been completed, she says again, a magnificent and well-balanced body of work. Ravel doesn't let her finish her sentence, interrupting her in despair: But how can you say that? I haven't written anything, I'm leaving nothing behind me, I haven't said anything of what I wanted to say.

He is alone in his house at Montfort, without any illusions. He has always been alone, but held aloft by music. Now he cannot stand his useless life anymore, rebels helplessly at no longer serving any purpose, at being locked up inside himself. Fully aware that it's all over, he tries to organize this solitude. Every day, after tramping through the forest of Rambouillet, which he still knows by heart in spite of his condition, he goes home to spend hours sitting expectantly by the telephone, hoping for a call from Édouard (who must often be away on business), still chainsmoking in spite of the doctor's orders, getting up to go empty the ashtray—a full ashtray is no less sad than an unmade bed. Every day as well, though, at five o'clock, he does get a visit from Jacques de Zogheb. As soon as Zogheb rings the doorbell, Ravel hurries to the door to try to open it. Since nothing in his body works anymore, his stiff fingers jerk the latch around in every direction and the bolt in the wrong one until he resigns himself to calling for his housekeeper. Through the door, Zogheb hears Ravel's increasingly frustrated curses answered by the desperate yapping of Mme Révelot until at last the door opens.

Zogheb takes Ravel by the arm; they go into the red-and-gray drawing room. Zogheb sits down on the sofa while Ravel lounges in an easy chair near the window. And every day it's the same dialogue. How are you? asks Zogheb. Poorly, says Ravel softly. Things are still the same. And when asked how he is sleeping, Ravel shakes his head. Any appetite? continues Zogheb. Appetite, yes, says Ravel distantly, some. And have you worked a little? Ravel shakes his head again, then tears well up suddenly, veiling his eyes. Why did this happen to me, he says. Why? Zogheb does not reply. Then, after a silence: Still, I'd written some things that weren't bad, hadn't I? Zogheb does not reply. He stays with Ravel until eight o'clock and the next day, at five, he returns to ask the same questions. Every day is the same until night falls and the question of sleep arises.

Technique Number 4: Potassium bromide, laudanum, veronal, nembutal, prominal, soneryl, and other barbiturates.

Objection: after serving him well, narcotics are now of very little help to him, they really don't do much anymore. Ravel does finally doze off, though, at the first glimmers of dawn. This interlude, however, brings only a troubled sleep disturbed by uneasy dreams that give him no rest: Ravel must confront monsters or even worse, escape from them. And it's at the worst moment of those struggles that he awakes with a start, worn out, each time more exhausted than the evening before, not even in a bad mood, not even in any mood.

It has taken some time but he is present when the *Piano Concerto for the Left Hand* is finally performed as it was written, stripped at last by Jacques Février of Wittgenstein's embellishments. During the concert, Ravel leans once more toward his neighbor to ask her if what they're listening to is really by him, although this time there is an extenuating circumstance: he had never heard it in that version. But when, three months later, he attends another concert devoted to his works for piano, he appears not to realize that he is the one being applauded at the end. He must think that these ovations are meant for an Italian colleague sitting next to him, for he turns to him politely with a rigid smile and frighteningly empty eyes. Then he is taken to dinner, going along without saying anything, a ghost as well-dressed as ever, except that on the lining of his jacket, in case of an emergency, Mme Révelot has taken care to pin his address.

Something must obviously be done; his friends discuss the situation constantly. In vain does Ida Rubinstein seek the advice of specialists in Switzerland, Germany, and England, who admit their perplexity. When two pioneers of brain surgery are consulted in Paris, one counsels against any intervention while the other says essentially that he wouldn't try anything either if the patient were just anyone, that the only thing to do would be to leave him in that state, though it would mean watching him endlessly fade away. But, well, it's Ravel. Given the situation, it would be better to try something. It is possible that a successful intervention would restore his faculties to him, offering him years of new creativity. Despite the results of examinations, which can always be unreliable, the hypothesis of a tumor might yet be considered and, from that point of view, he is willing to operate. Clovis Vincent is a famous neurosurgeon, one can only have confidence in him, his judgment proves persuasive, and the operation is scheduled for two days later.

Since Ravel's skull must be shaved beforehand, Édouard and the others try to reassure him when, seeing his hair falling, he begs to be taken home. They try to convince him that this is simply for another X-ray examination, some more extensive tests he must have, but Ravel doesn't believe any of it. No, no, he says faintly, I know they're going to slice up my noggin. Then while they enturban his head with white cloths, he seems to decide to make the best of it, the first one to smile at his unexpected resemblance to Lawrence of Arabia.

With bare hands and a saw, Dr. Vincent and his surgical team remove the right frontal panel of the skull, then open the dura mater transversely to see what's going on inside. They find a brain slightly shrunken on the left but of normal aspect otherwise, without any particular indication of softening even if the convolutions, not too atrophied either, are separated by some edema. Discovering no tumor, they puncture the ventricles to obtain a small amount of spinal fluid, which appears only when pressure is applied to the area. They inject a little water there several times in the hope of effecting a dilation; the brain swells but shrinks immediately: the cerebral atrophy seems irreversible, in short they haven't really gotten anywhere. Giving up, they close the site of the injection and, leaving the dura mater open, they replace the bone section, which they suture with brown thread.

After the operation, when Ravel regains consciousness for a moment, they think he has pulled through. He takes some nourishment, calls for Édouard, then asks to see a lady. They ask him which lady, suggesting names to him that he's unable to articulate. Ida Rubinstein? He gestures, no, pointing toward the floor. Hélène Jourdan-Morhange? No, he indicates. Marguerite Long? Not her at all, he signs through the same gesture. Lower, he says finally. Lower. They understand at last, and send for Mme Révelot. He goes back to sleep, he dies ten days later; they clothe his body in black tails, white vest, wing collar, white bow tie, pale gloves; he leaves no will, no image on film, not a single recording of his voice.

NOTES FROM THE TRANSLATOR

1. Hélène Jourdan-Morhange: A violinist, to whom Ravel dedicated his *Sonata for Violin and Cello*.
2. Orane Demazis: The actress who played Fanny in Marcel Pagnol's film trilogy set in 1930s Marseilles (*Marius,* 1931; *Fanny,* 1932; *César,* 1936).
3. Jacques de Zogheb: A writer in whose home Ravel met such literary figures as Colette, Paul Morand, and Jacques de Lacretelle.
4. Marcelle Gérar: The singer to whom Ravel dedicated *Ronsard à son âme*.

   Madeleine Grey: A noted interpreter of songs by Kurt Weill, De Falla, Villa-Lobos, and many others. Madeleine Grey premiered numerous works by Fauré and Milhaud, as well as Ravel's *Chansons madécasses* and *Deux mélodies hébraïques*.
5. The SS *Cap Arcona:* A German luxury ocean liner of the Hamburg–South America line. Launched in 1927, she was taken over by the German Navy in 1940. On April 26, 1945, loaded with prisoners from the Neuengamme concentration camp, she was sent into the Bay of Lübeck, where she was to be scuttled in an attempt to de-

stroy evidence of the atrocities at the camp. On May 3, 1945, although she hoisted the white ensign, the *Cap Arcona* was among several ships sunk in four separate attacks by RAF planes. Many survivors were shot by SS troops, while others were machine-gunned by British pilots.

6. Gerry Mulligan: One of the most versatile musicians in American jazz, a composer and arranger best known for his baritone saxophone playing.

7. Prix de Rome: A French scholarship created under the reign of Louis XIV that sent promising painters, sculptors, and architects to study in Rome. Musicians were allowed to compete after 1803. Ravel attempted five times to win the prize, and the scandal of "the Ravel Affair," his last failure in 1905, when he was favored to win, led to the reorganization of the administration at the Paris Conservatory.

8. *Ronsard à son âme* (*Ronsard to his soul*): A late Ravel song created for a late Ronsard poem, for voice and piano.

A son Ame	To His Soul
Amelette Ronsardelette,	Wee soul of mine, O Ronsardling,
Mignonnelette doucelette,	Thou fair, thou dulcet tiny thing,
Treschere hostesse de mon corps,	Dearest companion of my flesh,
Tu descens là bas foiblette,	Thou descendest now a weakling
Pasle, maigrelette, seulette,	Pallid, sole, and shriveling,
Dans le froid Royaume des mors:	To the cold Kingdom of death:
Toutesfois simple, sans remors	Simple yet, and sans remorse
De meurtre, poison, ou rancune,	For murder, poison, or rancors,
Méprisant faueurs et tresors	Treasure and favor thou despisèd
Tant enuiez par la commune.	Which the common man so prizèd.

Passant, i'ay dit, suy ta fortune	Traveler, hark, on thy fate wing
Ne trouble mon repos, ie dors.	And leave me be, here slumbering.

(Translation by Gilles Mourier)

9. Maurice Delage: One of Ravel's pupils and a distinguished composer. He and his wife Nelly were lifelong friends of Ravel's.

   Roland-Manuel: Roland Alexis Manuel Léoy, Belgian by birth, French composer and critic, stepson of Mme Fernand Dreyfus. Introduced to Ravel in 1911 by Erik Satie, he became Ravel's pupil and close friend.

10. Elie Robert Schmitz: A French pianist who lived much of his life in the United States. In 1920 he founded the Franco-American Society in New York, which became famous in 1923 under the name Pro Musica. The Pro Musica Society sponsored the first visits to America by Ravel, Bartók, and Respighi. It was Schmitz who conducted the premiere of *Boléro* for a dance recital by Ida Rubinstein.

11. Bolette Natanson: The daughter of Alexandre Natanson, one of the founders of the influential literary and artistic journal *La Revue blanche*. Bolette Natanson was one of the foremost designers in Paris in the 1940s.

12. Vincent Scotto: A French songwriter and composer of operettas and film music. Many of his songs were performed by Maurice Chevalier, Josephine Baker, and Edith Piaf.

    Noël-Noël: A cabaret singer and songwriter.

    Jean Tranchant: A popular cabaret singer.

13. René Kerdyck: A poet and writer whose works were published in very limited deluxe editions. He also wrote ballets, including *Beach*, presented in 1933 by Leonide Massine, performed by the Ballets Russes de Monte Carlo with décor by Raoul Dufy.

Pierre-Octave Ferroud: A French composer and critic.

Manuel Rosenthal: A pupil and friend of Ravel's, a conductor and composer who became best known for his lighter pieces, such as the ballet *Gaîté Parisienne*, based on the work of Jacques Offenbach. He was the longest-surviving close associate of Ravel, of whom he noted that the composer's most remarkable human quality was that "he never lied in his whole life, neither to his art, nor to his friends, nor to his enemies."

14. Ida Lvovna Rubinstein: A wealthy Belle Epoque beauty and an important figure in the arts during the first half of the century. Although she first appeared onstage in the Russian ballets by Diaghilev and studied with Sarah Bernhardt, Rubinstein was a mediocre dancer who carefully shaped her career by appearing as a dancer, mime artist, or actress in plays and ballets she commissioned from many of the leading artists of her day, including d'Annunzio, Debussy, Stravinsky, Gide, and Honegger.

15. Gustave Samazeuilh: A minor composer of vocal and instrumental works who was better known as a critic and translator. He had a house in Ciboure, where he befriended Ravel during the composer's summer holidays.

Marie Gaudin: Along with her sister Jane, the recipient of many letters from Ravel in which he shared his private thoughts and feelings. The Gaudins lived in Saint-Jean-de-Luz, and Ravel enjoyed a lifelong friendship with various members of the family. Marie and Jane's brother Edmond, who owned a car, would drive Ravel around the Basque country and to San Sebastián for the bullfights. Their brothers Pierre and Pascal both died during the First World War, and Ravel dedicated the "Rigaudon" section of his *Le Tombeau de Couperin* to them.

Joaquin Nin: A Cuban pianist and composer who was instrumental in renewing interest in the Argentine tango. He was the father of the writer Anaïs Nin and the concert pianist Joaquin Nin-Culmell.

16. *La Madelon:* A popular song about a cheerful and good-hearted waitress in a little country inn. The darling of lonely soldiers, Madelon refuses all their offers of marriage because she is too busy serving wine to the entire regiment.

17. Marguerite Long: France's foremost woman pianist during the first half of the twentieth century, who enjoyed an international career as a soloist and teacher. She premiered the *Piano Concerto in G Major* and *Le Tombeau de Couperin,* which last contained a section dedicated by Ravel to her husband, who was killed in the First World War.

18. *Jeanne d'Arc:* "Valentine, I will never compose my *Jeanne d'Arc*—that opera is there in my head, I hear it but I will never ever write it, it's over, I can no longer write my music." (Ravel in a letter to Valentine Hugo, November 1933.)

19. Robert Casadesus: A French pianist and composer who shared the concert stage with Ravel in England, France, and Spain. His recorded performances of Ravel's music are still highly prized. Renowned for his classical technique, he often performed with his wife, Gaby, and occasionally with both Gaby and their son, Jean.

20. Marcial Lalanda: The inventor of the *mariposa,* or "butterfly": a series of passes made by the torero with the cape over his shoulders, facing the bull and drawing him on by waving alternate sides of the cape, imitating the flight of a butterfly. In *Death in the Afternoon,* Hemingway writes of him, "As a complete, scientific torero he is the best there is in Spain."

Enrique Torres: In Hemingway's opinion, one of "the finest artists with the cape the ring has known."

Nicanor Villalta: "As awkward looking as a praying mantis any time he draws a difficult bull" because of his great height, according to Hemingway, but "everything he does he does bravely and everything he does he does in his own way."

In the Spanish press, the comments after the name of a matador or *novillero* refer, in order, to his performances with his first bull, second bull, and so on. Comments in order of precedence range from two symbolic ears and the tail (when the bull is pardoned for bravery); two ears and the tail; two ears; one ear; a turn around the ring; a standing ovation; hearty applause; salutations; polite applause; silence; whistles; vigorous protest. There can also be *division* of opinions on the part of the crowd.

21. *Minotaure:* A largely surrealist-oriented Parisian publication (1933–1939) that helped bring recognition to artists such as Roberto Matta, Alberto Giacometti, Paul Delvaux, and Hans Bellmer.

22. Valentine Hugo: A French artist, the wife of Jean Hugo, who was the great-grandson of Victor Hugo. She collaborated with her husband on ballet designs, including Jean Cocteau's *Les Mariés de la Tour Eiffel* (1921) and was the foremost illustrator of the poetry of Paul Éluard. Between 1930 and 1936, she was actively involved in the surrealist movement.

23. Paul Dukas: The composer of the infamous *Sorcerer's Apprentice.*

Charles Koechlin: A French composer who studied with Gabriel Fauré and strongly influenced Darius Milhaud, and whose distinguished teaching career brought him such pupils as Francis Poulenc and Germaine Tailleferre.

Other Novels by Jean Echenoz from The New Press

BIG BLONDES
Translated by Mark Polizzotti

Renowned singer Gloire Stella has mysteriously disappeared from the public eye. When a television documentary producer tries to track her down, Gloire goes on the run. *Big Blondes* chronicles her flight in a darkly comedic tour de force that probes our universal obsession with fame, taking a satiric yet chilling look at television stardom.

978-1-56584-340-0 (hc)
978-1-56584-447-6 (pb)

I'M GONE
Translated by Mark Polizzotti

Winner of the Prix Goncourt, this is the deceptively simple tale of a Parisian art dealer who abandons his wife and career to pursue a memorably pathetic international crime caper.

978-1-56584-628-9 (hc)
978-1-56584-746-0 (pb)

THE PIANO
Translated by Mark Polizzotti

A critically acclaimed bestseller in France, *Piano* tells the story of Max Delmarc, a famous concert pianist with two problems: the first, severe stage fright for which the second, alcohol, is the only cure. In this unparalleled comedy we journey with Max from the trials of his everyday life, to his untimely death, and on into the afterlife.

978-1-56584-871-9 (hc)

Other French fiction titles from The New Press

MAKING LOVE
Jean-Philippe Toussaint
TRANSLATED BY LINDA COVERDALE

Making Love is an original and daring retelling of a classic theme: the end of an affair. Following a couple's final days together in Japan, the novel explores the frustration of two lovers trying to break up with each other while on vacation, even as they go on a wild and intimate ramble through the streets of Tokyo.

978-1-56584-853-5 (hc)

PIG TALES
Marie Darrieussecq
TRANSLATED BY LINDA COVERDALE

Pig Tales is the story of a young woman who slowly metamorphoses into . . . a pig. What happens to her next overturns all our ideas about relationships between man, woman, and beast in a stunning fable of political and sexual corruption.

978-1-56584-361-5 (hc)
978-1-56584-442-1 (pb)

THE TROLLEY
Claude Simon
TRANSLATED BY RICHARD HOWARD

From the perch of a wheeled hospital bed, our narrator recalls the trolley that took him to and from school every morning of his childhood—passing back and forth between vine-covered hills, the shore, and the gradually modernizing town. When the past and present collide, the story becomes a fugue of memory that has delighted critics and made the book an immediate bestseller in France.

978-1-56584-734-7 (hc)
978-1-56584-857-3 (pb)